RED RAIN

ALSO IN THE RED RAIN SERIES

RED RAIN

RED RAIN #1

RACHEL NEWHOUSE

ISBN-13: 978-1-957432-02-1

Cover Art by Clarissa Laurenda (Instagram: @fungzauu_)
Cover Layout by Shawn Jonas
Illustrations by Shanalyse Barnett (shadowoodanimation.com)

This is a work of fiction. Any similarities to real people, living or dead, are merely coincidental.

Previously published under the penname Aubrey Hansen.

rachelnewhouse.com

To Grace
for being there
every step of the way

OCTOBER 2075

1

It had been almost six months since anyone had died because they refused to go to school.

Today, Mr. Dass was determined to break that record.

"Mr. Dass, need I use force?"

"You will need to use a lot more than force if you expect me to move!"

I cringed. Commander Ambrose shook his head. "Mr. Dass, I ask nothing unusual. Your children have been attending our school since—"

"Since you made them!" the red-faced father bellowed. He held his daughter Mira close to him. His son Stanyard stood safely behind him, fiddling with a backpack.

"A fair point." The commander shifted and cast his gaze around the street. All along the row of solid concrete homes, families stood in their doorways and watched. The bus, painted red with the harsh black words ASSIMILATION SERVICES on the side, idled in the road. The handful of kids inside pressed their faces against the windows; two armed guards leaned against the door. The driver tapped a small electric pistol on the wheel impatiently. No one else moved.

I fingered the pouch strapped around my waist. After the Dasses', our house across the street was the next—and last—stop.

I felt hands slide over my shoulders. I glanced up into my father's sober face. He rubbed my shoulders gently as he watched Mr. Dass.

Commander Ambrose spoke again. "You realize, Mr. Dass, that you are a civil criminal and in violation of United policy."

"By choice," Mr. Dass spat back.

"In the interest of preparing the younger generation to rejoin the United as productive members of society, your children must attend our school to be—"

"Indoctrinated against everything we've ever taught them!"

That's a decent way of summing it up.

My dad stopped rubbing, but he kept his hands on my shoulders. His eyes were closed.

Commander Ambrose tipped his head to the side. "Exactly." He looked down at Mira, who gazed up at him with wide dark eyes. Mr. Dass gripped his daughter's arms, as though daring the commander to rip her from his grasp.

The commander did. In one swift movement, he grabbed Mira's shoulders and yanked her from her father. Mira screamed, but the commander didn't hurt her. He shoved her down the steps and swung at Mr. Dass as the infuriated man dived. Mr. Dass stumbled but quickly regained his footing.

"You beast!" he snarled. He backed up, shielding his remaining child. "Just try and take my son."

"Are you enjoying this? Is this some sort of game to you?" the commander threatened.

Some days I wonder. My father pinched my shoulders.

There was silence, except for Mr. Dass's ragged breathing. The commander glared, but Mr. Dass didn't move. Finally, the commander drew his gun from his side.

I instinctively pinched my eyes shut. Daddy muttered under his breath, "Lord, not today."

There was scuffling. I opened my eyes to see Stanyard squeeze out from behind his father and scamper down the steps, head lowered. Wordlessly, he grabbed Mira's arm and hauled her onto the bus.

The commander watched them go, then turned back to Mr. Dass. The father's face was no longer red, but white.

"Your children are learning," Commander Ambrose said coolly, sliding his gun back in its holster. "They are smarter than your generation." And with that, he turned and marched across the street—towards us.

My father twisted me around to face him. Holding my shoulders, he bent low and spoke in quick whispers. "Remember why we always homeschooled. Believe nothing they say without comparing it to the Bible. Save all questions for home—tell me everything. Remember me, Philadelphia. Remember your mother. Remember God."

I nodded rapidly, staring into his brown eyes. He kissed my forehead and let me go; I ran down the steps and fled for the bus. The commander moved aside, one foot on the bottom step, to let me pass. He looked up at my father.

"Well, Dr. Smyrna, coming around, are we? You used to be the troublesome one."

My father straightened and said nothing. He watched me find a seat in the back of the bus. I waved through the window until we were out of sight.

The bus turned the corner and rumbled through another lane of houses, exactly the same as the street before. The houses were two-story concrete boxes with only three windows on the front. All of them were identical on both sides of the blacktop road. There were no trees, no grass, no mailboxes. Nothing personal about the yards whatsoever.

The only difference was the front doors, which were alternating colors going up the row—red, blue, orange, purple, green—to help separate the houses at a glance. Each house also had a number burned into the concrete step and plated on the door. My house number was 79.

There used to be exactly 110 houses in the Street 17 Containment Camp when it was first built five years ago. Five years ago, Street 17 camp was full, as were Street 80 and Street 83 camps.

Now my camp was down to 64 houses, and not all of them were occupied. The unused streets had been demolished and the concrete wall moved up, fencing the remaining houses in more closely.

It must have cost a fortune to rebuild the wall every other year, but I guess it was worth it to remind us that they were slowly crushing us out.

The bus stalled in front of the energized metal gates. A sensor in the wall scanned the license plate and blinked approvingly. The gates rolled back into the wall; the bus chugged through and waited until the gates shut themselves again. Then, for about ten minutes, the bus drove through the Outside.

I was glad we still lived in the camp across town. I enjoyed, however short, my ride through the Outside every day; I could look out the window freely and watch the world and its people. The trees, the grass, the signs—colorful display windows and strolling crowds. Unlike the camp, the Outside changed, shifted, bore new colors and new faces. The brief glimpse on the bus ride over was a relief, an entertainment—a reminder of what used to be.

I glanced across the aisle. Stanyard and Mira shared a seat there. Stanyard was leaning with his forehead against the seat in front of him, eyes glazed. Mira twisted her hands together.

"I'm sorry," I said.

Stanyard nodded wordlessly. Mira looked up at me. "He didn't hurt me," she assured.

Cami twisted around in the seat in front of me and looked back. "I'm surprised your father didn't offer any objections, Phil."

"How could he, after that?" her brother Aid quipped from beside her. "The commander hasn't pulled his gun in almost a month."

"We talked about it, last night," I mused. "He said it wasn't worth the blood right now."

"Smart man," Stanyard muttered. He sat up and gazed out the window. Mira stared straight ahead.

We went to the same public school all the regular kids attended. I suppose they were hoping that we'd see our peers—with their learner's permits and after-school jobs and shiny devices with unrestricted internet access—and want to join them.

It certainly seemed to be working. Our bus used to be a lot more crowded.

Although we attended the rest of our classes with the regular kids, our morning homeroom was a special "remedial" class headed by a teacher who, in his opinion, wasn't getting paid nearly enough to supervise the indoctrination of some religious brats. It was his job each morning to lecture us about the freedoms we could have if we would just get with the program and sign over our right to religious expression.

He treated it as such a trivial thing, like we were giving up our right to choose what color of socks we wore. If we would simply succumb to a little conformity in the name of peace and equality, we could rejoin society with all the rights owed to us as full United citizens.

I never watched his face during his tirades; if I looked at something else, filled my mind with anything else, it made his voice sound smaller. I often looked at the projections on the wall, toyed with the cursor on my laptop, or prayed.

I never, ever looked out the windows. I never, ever looked at the Outside—the freedom I would gain if I followed my teacher's words.

The rest of the school day wasn't much better. Math was my favorite subject, although not because I was particularly good at it; they just seemed to waste less time trying to squeeze propaganda into trigonometry than they did with other subjects.

History was the worst. It was nothing like the stories my grandpa used to tell me; all of the glorious and inglorious escapades of humanity had been stripped and sanitized and manipulated. Every era now existed exclusively to demonstrate the need for the United.

According to our textbook, the United was humanity's greatest achievement. It was the solution to every war, every injustice, every inequality. The glories of the United were raved to us as our teachers reveled in the progress of the one-mind, one-body megacountry the world was slowly forming. Segments all over the globe were dropping their boundaries and cultural differences and assimilating into a homogenized body that was its own god.

And of course, it was stressed that religion was a major hindrance to progress in the United. A hindrance that must be assimilated or removed.

Philadelphia

2

The bus was quiet on the way home. I sat by myself and thumbed through the Bible on my reader. I skimmed the virtual pages, picking up random verses.

My times are in your hands... deliver me... from those who pursue me...

I jumped when Cami slipped across the aisle and squeezed in next to me. I looked at her face and instantly knew what she was going to ask.

"Can you?"

I held out my hand. She pressed a tiny chip into my palm.

I closed my window and snapped the chip into my reader. The screen chirped.

Cami explained while I navigated my library to find the appropriate file. "The Marksens, the new people, had their data wiped."

"Weren't they caught transmitting?"

"Yeah. Apparently the father signed the file to keep his job, but the kids hadn't. Or something. But they lost all their data."

She picked at the peeling vinyl bench with her fingernail. "Dad wanted me to ask you to do it."

I didn't need an explanation. I knew why I always made the copies, even though Cami's reader was perfectly capable. Everyone else stopped making copies after my mother died.

I suppose they stopped for the same reason my father kept doing it—and kept letting me do it. Even if his wife had died for violating the "no transmitting" law.

I suspected the commander knew what I was doing. After all, my device was continually connected to either the camp or school wifi. He could monitor my activity if he wanted to. I assumed he didn't care, not if I limited my distribution to my fellow inmates. We were all criminals anyway.

I knew he would care if he found out my dad was transmitting copies from work.

"Thanks," Cami said finally.

I nodded and tapped the screen. The progress bar seemed stuck at 15%. Usually it took about three seconds, five if my dinosaur of an electronic was feeling grumpy.

"Something wrong?" Cami asked, probably more worriedly than she intended.

"It's stuck. I'm going to try again." I canceled the transfer and backed out to the main menu. I clicked on the Bible folder and got a hideous beep. I shuddered and looked at the screen.

It said: *File not found.*

I frowned and backed out a few folders, then went in another way. This time, I couldn't even find the folder.

"What's wrong?"

"It's gone."

"What?"

"My Bible—the file. It's gone."

Cami snatched her reader out of her bag. She flicked it on and thumbed for a minute.

I squinted at her screen. "Bible" was missing from the alphabetical list of folders.

She stared at me dumbly.

I leaned forward and hissed across the aisle. "Mira!"

She glanced in my direction. Stanyard continued to stare out the window.

"Open your laptop."

"Why?"

"See if your Bible is still there."

"Why would it—"

"Just do it!" Cami squeaked. She chewed on a sprig of her hair.

Mira obeyed. Aid glanced back at us, frowning. He quickly opened a new window on his tablet.

"The file's gone," Mira reported.

"Can't find it." Aid tapped through more menus.

"I still have my study notes," Mira offered. Stanyard finally sat up and turned to face us.

"I'm missing some stuff for school, too," Aid said. "Some essays. The folder's there, but a few of the files are gone."

"Are you sure you downloaded them at school?" Stanyard questioned.

"Yeah." Aid flopped back in his seat and stared profoundly at his screen.

An idea hit me. I quickly scrolled through the menus, hoping. A second later I proved myself wrong. "It's not in trash, either."

"We'll have to recopy it from school tomorrow, I guess," Mira said.

"They don't have a Bible on the school's cloud," Cami reminded her.

"My dad does." I straightened. "I'll get a copy from him and upload it."

Cami just nodded.

"Freaky glitch," Aid suggested. Stanyard scrunched his eyebrows.

A glitch... just a bug. I slid my reader into my pouch and smoothed the flap, praying. It was just a glitch.

3

As soon as I got home, I checked the household desktop. The file was nowhere to be found.

I tried not to let that worry me. After all, my reader and the home computer both stored their data on the same cloud. If it was a glitch in the system, all the devices in the camp would be affected.

Cami came running to my house a half-hour later to confirm that fact.

I tried to make myself useful until Dad got home. He realized something was up the minute he walked in the door, so I told him.

He searched his work tablet. Nothing.

"I'll check at work," he said.

The next evening, he reported that all the copies he had on his work computer were gone. The ones he had uploaded to the United web were missing too. It was as if someone had gone through and deleted them all.

I prayed that didn't mean the government had found them.

Daddy said he'd ask around. For three days he searched, and for three days I tried to reestablish normalcy, half-expecting United officers to show up at the door citing Section 10.20.08 about the high crime of transmitting.

They never did. Daddy didn't find any Bibles, either. He looked at all the transmitting sites he knew of. All of them were down or blank.

On Friday, he finally brought something home. But it wasn't a Bible—it was a copy of an official statement by the United.

In it, they claimed they were not responsible for the virus and an investigation was being conducted.

The statement didn't say anything about the Bible. Daddy finally explained everything.

It was a virus. Someone had released a virus onto the United web that was attacking large chunks of data, permanently deleting or corrupting the information in seconds. It was miscellaneous data that had no apparent connection. Random entries missing from directories, blog posts and web pages that had vanished, sporadic issues deleted from magazine archives. And books. Thousands of books were wiped from the virtual libraries. The Bible was among them.

I wondered if that was intentional.

Daddy didn't think so. He said that if the United wanted to destroy all the Bibles as an attack on religion, they would have made a demonstration out of it. They would have deleted just the Bible and not crippled the entire system with a badly-programmed virus.

But who else would want to delete the Bible?

Perhaps it didn't matter. It was done. As near as they could tell, the virus had originated on a social media site, which meant that before anyone knew it existed, millions of devices had already contracted and spread it. And since every device was legally required to be connected to wifi through an approved carrier at all times, we could only assume the Bible was gone on every cloud from here to Mars.

Daddy said the Bible wasn't lost forever. It was hard to permanently erase data, he explained. They would find a copy burned on a chip, or maybe stored on a server that wasn't connected to wifi. Those were illegal, but surely they existed. Even the government itself probably had a copy on a secure database somewhere.

But I knew finding a copy wasn't the problem. The problem was distributing it. To share it, we'd have to upload it to the United web, and that was illegal. Would the United recall their "no transmitting" law to appease a bunch of criminals?

I doubted it.

4

I failed miserably at school all week. For the first few days, I woke up promptly at 6:30 for my Bible study—only to find I had nothing to study.

On Saturday, I stared at the list of files on my reader. On Sunday, I got up and tried to do something else, but I ended up on the kitchen floor in a sea of broken glass, weeping.

Monday was the worst. I sat at my desk and tried to reconstruct some verses from my study notes. For some reason mine hadn't been affected by the virus, though Cami had lost most of hers.

The exercise hurt more than it helped. I ended up with one page of verses, half of which I knew were paraphrases.

Daddy said I would remember more later, when I was in a clearer frame of mind.

I wondered if I would ever have a clear head again.

As soon as we walked into homeroom Tuesday, our teacher started herding us into a line. "Hurry up—the principal wants to see you."

He lined us up and inspected us. He sent Stanyard to wash his face and Cami to redo her ponytail. He gestured for Aid to stand up straight, then snapped his fingers in front of Mira's face to wipe the glazed look from her eyes. When he came to me, he tugged at the corners of his lips.

I forced a smile.

He returned it. "Respectable."

The principal divided us up and sent us into different meeting rooms. Mira and Stanyard went to Room 1, Cami and Aid to Room 2. I was sent alone to Room 3.

The principal shut the door behind me. At first I thought the room was empty, but someone suddenly stood up from a chair against the wall and walked towards me.

"Oh, Philadelphia, is it?"

Cropped blond hair bobbed around her face. Her lips were bright red and her cheeks were painted pink. She stopped in front of me and smiled broadly.

"Hello," I managed.

"Sweet voice!" she crooned. She rubbed her chin and examined me. "Hmm... They told me so much about you. You're better than they described!"

Better in what way?

She didn't explain. She just hugged me.

I wanted to pull away, but for some reason, I didn't. She squeezed me and then stepped back, arm around my shoulder. "I'm Mrs. Nolan. Delighted to finally meet you! Come, sit by me."

She led me across the room, and I did as I was told—stiffly.

"The school told me all about you. They described all the kids to us, but when I heard about 'Philadelphia,' I knew you were the one I wanted to meet. My husband agreed. You sounded perfect for us! Just the right age, calm disposition..."

I couldn't help it. "Perfect for us, ma'am?"

"Us—my husband and I. Just us, only kid is grown, so we have the spare bedroom, all ready for you. We're going to have it painted this weekend, unless you'd like navy walls? I was going to ask you what color you might like instead."

"Walls, ma'am?"

"I love how you call me 'ma'am'! Yes, walls. Bedroom walls. Your bedroom walls!" She grabbed her purse off the chair and fumbled with the zipper. "Do you want to see pictures? I have pictures of our street, the house... and the cat!"

"No, ma'am, I want to know why I need a bedroom."

She smiled. I decided she was enjoying the backwards conversation. "To sleep in, darling!"

I caught on. I was 16, old enough to work. Being assigned a job was not an unreasonable expectation. "That will be unnecessary, ma'am."

She laughed. "Oh, do you have other arrangements?"

"If I work for you, I will come home to the camp at night."

"Work? If you want a job, we can manage that later. There will be plenty of options available to you outside the home. I don't need a maid!"

"All assignments for unassimilated individuals must be approved by Commander Ambrose," I recited, for once finding solace in the rigidness of the law.

"When you're living in my house, that won't be necessary."

I looked her straight in the face. She stared back, coyness gone. Bluntly, "We want you to join our family."

I sank back in the chair.

"The school has been seeking loving United families to adopt the unassimilated children. We will take you into our family, make you ours, shelter you while you absorb into the real world..."

Assimilated or removed. Assimilated or removed.

"The officials talked to us, and we were eager to be a part of this program. I just loved your description! And now that I've met you, I know we'll manage beautifully. I'll bring Mr. Nolan by tomorrow—"

"I'm afraid I can't come, ma'am."

"Don't be so quick to pass it off! This is a unique program, sweetheart. We will ease you into reality, instead of dumping you on the street as an adult. You've had a difficult life away from the real world. This is your chance to come in, gently…"

"The real world won't accept me, ma'am. I won't sign the file."

"Is that it? I grieve for you, sweetheart."

She sighed. That was the end of the conversation for me, but it wasn't for her.

"They won't make you—I won't make you," she mused, looking elsewhere. "I don't want to force you into our family. But we want you, Philadelphia. We don't care about your past. We want to see you have a life before you—a real life! In the real world! We want you. Come out. Come out while you have open arms waiting for you."

I closed my eyes and thought of the open arms waiting for me at home.

When I opened my eyes, Mrs. Nolan was staring at me again. Her gaze was dark.

I got up and left unbidden.

She called to me when I reached the door. "You will have to sign the file eventually. You know you will. Take my offer while you can. Think about it, Philadelphia. Think about it."

I decided to never think of it again.

5

I wasn't able to talk to my friends until we were seated on the bus. I glanced across the aisle and instantly noticed how pale Aid's face was.

"Outsiders?" I suggested.

Aid nodded wordlessly.

"I hate them!" Cami screeched.

"Cam, hate's evil. That's what got us contained in a camp," Aid muttered.

Cami continued her tirade. "How could they! Assigning us families... I'm not going! I didn't listen to a word she said. Or he said."

"No one's going to make us go," Aid told her. "We'll tell Dad, and if they ask to see us again, we'll refuse."

Cami nodded, but her lip trembled.

I looked up the row at Mira and Stanyard. "You too?"

Mira nodded distantly.

"How were they?"

Mira shrugged. Stanyard wasn't listening.

"What about you, Philli?" Cami leaned across the aisle.

I looked out the window. "I wonder how much she knew about me before coming."

"Too much," was Aid's opinion.

"How was she?"

"Buttery." I thought. "Compromising."

＊

"Daddy, you're home early," I declared as I walked in the door.

He pushed his computer away from him. "I've been home almost all day. I had a special meeting at the lab—that's it."

I sat down next to him at the table. "They had 'special meetings' today at school, too."

He noted my frown. "What is it, Phil?"

He stared at me quietly while I told him about Mrs. Nolan.

When I was done, he shook his head. "I'm sorry, Phil."

"I love you, Daddy."

"My meeting wasn't much more pleasant. I was told that I've received a commission to work on a special project—requested by name, they tell me."

I tipped my head. That sounded like good news.

Daddy got up and started to pace.

It wasn't good news.

"The assignment… is for a base on Mars."

I wasn't sure what to make of that.

"And you would not be permitted to come with me."

I looked up into his face. He was already staring at me.

"The commander says. 'Regulations.' The assignment is for me, not you."

"Where… would I go?"

"Nowhere." Daddy folded his arms behind his back. "I will not go, I will not take the commission. Philadelphia, I will not leave you." He drew a breath and added, "Not if I have a choice."

I looked away. My eyes fell on the picture frame hanging on the wall across the room. I got up and walked over to it. The image displayed a picture of Daddy and me; Daddy usually left that one up, because it didn't hurt to look at it.

I waved my hand in front of the sensor several times. The digital pictures scrolled slowly, dancing through a time-lapse. I stopped when I reached the picture I was looking for.

I stepped away, crossed my arms behind my back, and regarded the photo. In the plain metal frame sat a young man, fresh out of college. His thick dark hair stuck up in the front, and his lab coat was pulled around his shoulders. He stared calmly at the camera, not smiling—the smile was in his eyes. I knew; I had grown up with my older brother's eyes smiling on me.

"They sent Ephesus to Mars," I said aloud.

"Yes," my father replied.

"They didn't give him a choice."

"No."

I stared hard at the image of my brother's face, wishing the pixels could move. Finally I finished my thought.

"And he never came back."

It was several minutes before my father replied. "No," he said finally. And again, "No, he didn't."

Dr. Smyrna

6

When I arrived in my classroom Thursday morning, I was told to head straight to the principal's office. Without stopping to explain, the principal shoved me into a meeting room and shut the door behind me. Mrs. Nolan was waiting.

She sat on one of the boring metal chairs, fingering a tablet computer. She looked up at me and smiled warmly. "Ah, Philli, you're here."

I crossed my arms behind my back. I wasn't sure whether to sit, stand, or inform the lady that I didn't want to talk to her. What I really wanted to tell her was that she didn't have any right to use my nickname. But I knew my father would want me to be somewhat polite.

"I hope you're well, ma'am," I said, voice proper.

Her eyes twinkled. "'Ma'am,' again? You're such a sweet and well-behaved child. I love your mannerisms!" She gestured at the chair across from her. "Do sit down."

I gingerly did so, adjusting my skirt. I sat on my fingers to keep them from clenching. Mrs. Nolan leaned across and touched my knee.

"I wanted to talk to you about my offer."

"Thank you, ma'am, but I haven't changed my mind," I said quickly, trying to keep the terseness out of my voice.

"I know, sweetheart, but I had an idea that might prove satisfactory to you. What if you came and stayed at my house, just for a week? Then you could see the world, try life out here, you know? You might change your mind if you had a chance to experience it…"

"I'm sorry, ma'am, but I can't do that."

Mrs. Nolan was not deterred. She looked at me for a moment, then squeezed my knee. Her voice lost its butter; it was firm, but not hard. "You're scared, aren't you?"

I blinked. She held my gaze.

"You think coming outside will mean giving up your religion, don't you?"

"I have been informed that, to be fully assimilated, I must sign a file officially denying my right to expression of religion," I recited emotionlessly.

Mrs. Nolan nodded. "True enough, most of the time. But, darling, I have an offer for you."

I steeled my nerves. Each of her "offers" had been more disagreeable than the last.

"If you come to my house, you may keep your Bible. You may pray and worship however you like in your room, and no one will bother you."

I frowned. "Those found supporting and hiding observers of religion are subject to like punishment, ma'am."

Mrs. Nolan smiled coyly. "You underestimate the power of money, darling. Money can buy many things, and one of them is privacy. My husband is well spoken of with the commander; they have agreed on the terms. You do not need to sign the file to join our family—special exception just for you. Come with me, Philadelphia, and you can keep your Bible in peace." She leaned closer to me. "Come with me."

I scooted back on the chair. "I don't have a Bible anymore," I mumbled. "It was lost in the virus."

Mrs. Nolan straightened. "Then what do you have to lose?" She held me in her gaze.

Suddenly, I looked away.

She took her hand off my knee. I jumped up and ran for the door. Mrs. Nolan's voice called out to me. "Think about it, Philadelphia, think about it."

I hesitated, gripping the door handle. Then I yanked the door open and fled the room.

I slid through the principal's office before she could speak to me. I stumbled around the halls until I found a deserted side wing. Sinking down on the cold concrete, I hid my face and wept.

*

"What did the principal want you for, Philli?"

"Yeah, what's up? Did you do something wrong?"

I looked away, out at the barren school lot surrounded by electric fences. "I did nothing wrong."

Cami wouldn't accept that for an answer. She placed herself in my line of vision. "Your face is red," she informed me. "You've been crying. You were incredibly distant during class. Do you even realize you failed the quiz?"

I shrugged, clutching my reader to my chest. "I'll retake it tomorrow."

Mira joined the chase now. She pinched my arm. "Philli, what's wrong? You can trust us." She gestured at the kids gathered loosely around.

"Come on, Phil," Aid said, "tell us." The group murmured their agreement.

I wiggled out of Mira's grasp. "Mrs. Nolan wanted to talk to me again. That's all."

"Your Outsider?" Aid guessed.

"She's not mine. It was nothing important."

"Nothing important!" Cami squawked. "She must like you if she came back again. What did she want?"

"She just wanted to make sure I hadn't changed my mind," I said dismissively.

"And that made you cry?" Stanyard snorted.

"Stanyard, be respectful!" Aid snapped.

Stanyard backed away, shrugging carelessly. "I don't see what would have gotten Phil worked up, that's all."

"Well, Outsiders came to see you again today, too. What did they want, huh?" Cami planted her hands on her hips.

Stanyard looked away. "They just wanted to talk more." He shifted his backpack; it looked lumpier than usual.

"I doubt it!" Cami cried. "I had to take a laptop to the principal's office, and I saw you talking to her. You too, Mira." Cami turned on Mira. "What were you doing, huh? And why do you have two bags today?"

Mira wouldn't meet her gaze. She stepped in front of the extra duffle she had set next to her backpack, as though she could hide it.

"Ha, you're avoiding me! *Mira*," Cami's voice changed to a begging wail, "what's up? Please?"

Mira shared a glance with her brother. Then she turned back to us and admitted, "We're going home with them today."

The group gasped. I couldn't find any air to gasp with; I just paled.

Mira scanned the group, and her fists tensed. "We're not going to do it anymore! We're leaving! We're not going to keep living stuffed away in a little hole until they decide to kill us. We accepted their offer, Stan and I. We agreed on it last night. They'll be here to pick us up any minute."

Stanyard nodded his consent. His face was hard.

"Then you... denied Him," I said flatly.

"We signed the file saying we wouldn't practice a religion anymore, yes." Mira shrugged as though it had no effect. "We figure they can't stop us from thinking about it, and that's what matters, right? It's a relationship, not a religion. The Bibles are gone, anyway."

"You... denied Him," I said again.

"It's the only way," Stanyard spat. "If you were smart, you'd do it too." His voice suddenly lowered, and he looked directly at me. "Take their offer while you still can, Phil—take it and run."

"But what about your parents?" Cami finally found her voice.

"We didn't tell them," Mira admitted. "I left a note this morning."

"This will kill your father, I can assure you," Aid declared.

"He's going to kill himself!" Stanyard shouted back. "He'll come out soon enough, when he realizes the truth."

I am the way, the truth... I watched them. Mira wouldn't look at me anymore.

A horn screeched. The bus pulled through the gates, followed by a little car. It was a normal silver four-door, driven by a normal mother and a normal father. The bus parked in its usual spot along the fence, but the car swerved up to us. The man and woman got out and walked towards our group.

"Mira? Stan?" the woman said hopefully. The brother and sister scooped up their baggage and walked towards the couple. The woman hugged and kissed them both. The man shook Stanyard's hand and patted his shoulder.

"Are you ready to go?" he asked.

The siblings nodded. "Yes, sir," Mira said.

"And thank you," Stanyard added.

The woman beamed. "It's our pleasure. Come on, our son is dying to meet you. Welcome home." The woman put her arm around Mira's shoulders and led her towards the car, chattering warmly. Mira did not look back.

The bus honked. The other kids fled towards its open doors; I stayed, rooted where I was.

Stanyard dropped his bag in the trunk and slammed it shut. He walked around to the backseat and stood with his hand on the door handle. I begged him to turn around; mentally I pleaded with him to change his mind. He abruptly glanced back at me, eyes filled with ice.

"Accept their offer while you still can." Then he got in the car and shut the door.

"Girl, if you're not going with them, you'd better come with us," the bus driver barked. I took one step backwards. The father looked up at me as he slid into the driver's seat.

"We'd take another," he said with a wink.

I turned and bolted for the bus doors.

7

Daddy wasn't home when I trudged off the bus. I waited for him in the living room until it was time to make dinner, but he never came. I managed to swallow a little something, then sat and fidgeted. Finally, at nearly 23:00, he opened the front door.

"Daddy!" I cried as soon as I heard the handle turn.

He didn't look at me as he slid around the door, locking it behind him. He kicked off his shoes and shrugged his lab coat from his shoulders. He dropped it across the back of the couch and then sat down, beckoning to me.

"Philli, we need to talk."

I sat down next to him. "Daddy, I know, it's Mira, and—"

My father shook his head. "No, Philli, I need to..." He looked into my face for the first time. "What's the matter? You're red."

I rubbed my arm across my cheek. "Did you have something you wanted to say first?"

"Yes," he said a little too quickly, then caught himself. "No, but it can... I think you had best tell me what's wrong."

I glanced at my white hands, wondering what to tell him first.

"Did something happen here, or was it at school?"

"At school," I replied, "and... Mira and Stanyard left." There, at least I was out with half of it.

"Left?" my father repeated, even though he knew what I meant.

"They went home with an Outsider family today," I said quietly.

My father pondered this before replying. "Of their own free will?"

"They agreed amongst themselves."

"And their parents?"

I shook my head. "They didn't tell them. We only found out after school while waiting for the bus."

My father groaned and sank back as far as the thin couch cushions would let him. He dragged his fingers through his hair, then held still for a minute. Eventually, he dropped his arms and looked back up at me. "Is that all?"

I swallowed. "No."

Daddy shifted so he was sitting up straight. "What else?"

I drew in a long breath. "Mrs. Nolan came to see me again."

Daddy let out his breath in a low sigh. "And what did she say?"

"She wanted to make sure I hadn't changed my mind... which I hadn't."

Daddy nodded.

"And... she offered me the chance to stay at her house for a week, just to 'try' it. I said no." I looked into Daddy's eyes for approval; there was none, less or more. "Aren't you glad I declined? Daddy?"

"What else?" he said, ignoring my question.

A clammy feeling rose up in my palms. I glanced down and dug my fingers into my skirt. "She... she said I could... She offered me the option to... keep my Christianity."

I looked up at his face suddenly; his expression was dead. I blundered through the rest of the tale.

"She said that her husband, who is important and rich or something, has spoken with the commander, Daddy, and they agreed that I could keep my faith... Daddy, she wouldn't make me sign the file. I could pray, worship—in the privacy of my room, and no one would bother me. Daddy, she offered me... freedom, Daddy, tolerance. She said I could go and not have to deny Christ!" My voice wobbled.

Daddy still said nothing. He blinked once. My jaw vibrated, but I forced the words out.

"And, Daddy... there's more. Daddy, I... I believed her. It sounded... so nice, so peaceful, a compromise, you know? With the Bibles already gone, there's no physical token, and if I don't have to sign the file..."

Daddy suddenly looked away. His crestfallen look broke my heart. My words gushed.

"Daddy, Daddy, I'm sorry! I know... I know it wasn't right, I know! I know she's just trying to convince me. Maybe she isn't lying, maybe she really won't make me sign the file, but, Daddy," I reached out to him, "I know she's just trying to get me to come. I know, it's compromise, and compromise is dangerous. Daddy, I know! I'm sorry! Daddy!"

He didn't turn to look at me. I shook in silence. When he didn't answer for a long minute, I dared to whisper, "Dad?"

He sighed. His voice was gently reassuring—not at all mad or disappointed. "I understand, Philli, I really do."

The quiver vanished from my nerves, leaving a watery feeling in their place. He thought for a minute before speaking again. "And... I'm glad you think that way."

"Daddy!" I screeched. My father, glad I was tempted by the Outside? I felt betrayed; never before had my father condoned anything from the Outside.

"I'm glad," he explained, still avoiding my eyes, "that you aren't repulsed by this family. I'm glad they like you. I'm glad they've offered you some tolerance. Because..." Finally he looked at me. "I want you to accept their offer, Phil."

"Daddy!" I wailed again, jolting upright. No other word could express my emotion. Now I felt betrayed—and abandoned.

"Philadelphia, it's the only way!" My father's voice rose to a terrified shout. He abruptly stood up and started pacing around the room. "I was informed today that, since I'm 'unassimilated,' I have no choice. I must accept the mission and go to Mars. I leave Monday morning. And you are not permitted to come with me."

He stopped pacing with his back to me. "I want you to send an email to your principal and tell her that you accept the Nolans' offer. You will stay with me for the rest of the week—you won't go to school tomorrow whatever they say—and join the family on Monday when I leave."

My father whipped around to face me. Helpless tears were streaming down his face. It took me a minute to realize silent rivers were coursing down my own cheeks too. "Don't apologize, Philli! *I'm* sorry! There's nothing I can do... nothing!"

I ran for him. He caught me in his arms and wailed openly. I could find no sound to utter—only bitter, drowning, ugly tears.

8

Monday morning found us standing on the step like we always did.

Only this time, we were alone on the street. Daddy's escort was scheduled to pick him up at 6, two hours before my bus would come.

For those two hours I would be completely alone. Two hours of interim, ripped from one family before being assimilated into another.

It was selfish, but I wished Daddy didn't have to leave until after I was gone. Then he could wave to me as I left, and we could pretend, just for a moment, that it was a normal school day and I'd be back in the evening.

But maybe that would have hurt even worse.

"Behave. Be polite," Daddy said after we'd nursed the silence for several minutes. "Obey the rules. Don't cause trouble."

I nodded, not trusting my voice to respond.

He kissed my forehead. "If I come back, I will find you." He was honest and used the word "if."

I hugged him and prayed, feeling tears and not caring whether they fell or not.

I wasn't unhappy that Commander Ambrose was fifteen minutes late. He finally drove up in a small armored car.

He got out and gestured with his pistol. "Get in." A guard emerged from the car and scooped Daddy's luggage off the sidewalk.

Daddy stooped to my eye level. "Remember me. Remember your mother. Remember God." We hugged one last time.

Then he picked up his carry-on and walked down the steps. The tears finally broke as a sob escaped my lips. I prayed louder, mentally scrambling for appropriate last words.

The commander interrupted the whirlwind. "Hurry up."

I glanced at Daddy, but the commander wasn't talking to him. He was looking at me.

Panic gripped my throat. No, it wasn't panic.

The commander repeated his order slowly. "Come on."

Daddy stopped and looked back at us. The commander jabbed his pistol at me. "Get in."

I slapped a hand over my mouth.

"You've been ordered to attend your father."

*

The world was oblivious of us. And it felt wonderful.

Masses of people crowded the port, joining lines and breaking them. Planes and transits crossed paths, bringing passengers from as far away as Neptune and as nearby as the city next over. A dizzying array of signs and status boards attempted to make sense of the mess.

Daddy and I pushed through the crowd. No one noticed us, no one bothered us. No one knew we were unassimilated—no one cared. We were simply passengers rushing to make our flight, just like everyone else.

The only person that paid us any mind was Commander Ambrose. He escorted us to our transit, armed with a pistol for show. He briskly stormed through the crowd, shoving people out of his way. Daddy ran to keep up with him.

I clutched Daddy's hand to keep from getting separated. That was the only thing I cared about.

We finally reached our terminal. A long line of people snaked out of the security gates—a splash of tourists, some businessmen, and a handful of regular people going up to populate.

There were more scientists than anything else. I wondered how many—if any—were going to our base.

I didn't know exactly where we were going. I doubted Daddy knew either. All Commander Ambrose had told us was that the governor of a base—he called him Dr. Nic—wanted Dad to work for him. And that was all the information Commander Ambrose thought was necessary. We would have to wait and find out more when we arrived.

But I didn't care what base we were going to. The only thing I cared about was that I was going with Daddy. We were together, and that was all I needed to know.

I wasn't sure what had changed. I highly doubted the commander had changed his mind out of pity. Commander Ambrose wouldn't say, just that it was an official order—from somebody.

But then again, everything was an "official order" with Commander Ambrose.

I didn't really care how it had come to pass. God can use whatever method He pleases to make things happen.

We cleared security and confirmed our tickets by pressing our thumbs to a scanner. The positive green light we received was comforting.

Commander Ambrose had a word with an officer, who gave us a frown and assisted us to the transit. Daddy glanced back once; I followed his gaze.

Commander Ambrose stood on the other side of security, arms crossed. He scowled until the crowd swallowed him up.

I turned around. I prayed that maybe, just maybe, I would never see him again.

The transit was like a plane bloated with air. The seats were farther apart, and the ceiling swooped high overhead like a bowl. The whole place seemed fancier, more luxurious—glitzy, shiny, well-padded—than the last airplane I had seen.

The officer led us down the carpeted main aisle and into a room filled with chairs. The seats weren't lined up in strict rows but rather scattered around in clusters with tables mixed in. A handful of passengers milled about, chattering and laughing like guests at a party.

Daddy and I sat near the door; the officer waited beside us. I watched the other passengers flow in and scatter; soon the room was filled with people. The final call for passengers echoed over the speakers. The officer told us the number of our cabin and informed us that another officer would "assist" us when we docked. Then he left.

We were free. For the next 59.5 hours, we were no different than any other passenger on the transit.

We were normal.

Somewhere deep beneath my feet, a rumble began to churn. A computerized voice over the speakers calmly instructed us through the basic rules of safety, then commanded everyone to take a seat while we launched. We obeyed. Every seat in the room was full, as far I could see.

The rumble surged. There were no seatbelts—I had a tiny fear that there should be something restraining me—but Daddy held my hand. The room went quiet briefly; chatter ceased while a high-pitched whir joined the rumble. A sound like air rushing down a huge tunnel streamed past the walls of the transit. I felt the ship turn, slightly.

Then the rumble and whir silenced to a muted grind. The speakers announced a successful take-off, and the noise of people erupted. The passengers resumed chatting and began to disperse.

We were flying.

We had left Earth.

And maybe, just maybe, we would never come back.

9

After the room thinned, Daddy got up to explore the accommodations. He left me with the instructions to stay put and be discreet. It was okay if I talked with people, told them my name and who my father was, and why we were going to Mars.

But I should tell no one that I was unassimilated.

He whispered in my ear, "'My father has received a scientific assignment on Mars' should be sufficient for most people. If they ask for more, they don't need to be answered. I assume the governor of the base already knows, but..." At this point, he sighed. "There's no reason to cause trouble and division where it isn't needed."

After he left, I moved to a more secluded spot in an empty circle of chairs. I climbed into the seat against the wall, tucking my legs under me. There were no windows, which I suppose was for the better. Earth would be shrinking so quickly, left far behind by our great speed, that the view probably would have been dizzying.

I slid my reader from its pouch. I rubbed the scratched case for a moment before turning it on. I watched the screen light up and spew off a random string of code that probably said, *"Good morning! My systems are in good shape and I'm waking up."*

As soon as the welcome screen flickered on, I remembered that I had nothing to read. All of my books had been stored on the camp's cloud, and I hadn't bothered to copy most of them over. Most of my books were from the United, things I only read because my teacher made me. But he couldn't make me read anything now, so why take the files with me?

I had copied over my Bible study notes. I wondered if it would be safe to paw through them and look for traces of verses. I voted against doing it in a public room—maybe when we got back to the cabins. I had a whole file of jumbled verses to organize in order when I had privacy.

Daddy had been compiling them. He wrote down a chunk every night. I had given up trying to think of many verses myself, but I reformatted the ones Daddy remembered, engraving them in my brain as I did so.

I imagined the phrases of Scripture forming across the screen, echoed by the comforting clack of keystrokes. The pages would fill...

But it would be a long time before we regenerated all 1,000 of them.

Or even 100 pages.

And then again, our devices would probably be monitored when we got to the base. Would typing up a file of verses count as transmitting? Commander Ambrose didn't care, but this Dr. Nic might.

The welcome screen sat waiting. I mindlessly clicked on the menu and watched the list of files generate.

Someone disturbed my solace. A 20-something gingerly eased into the chair across from me. She tucked her short blond curls behind her ears and glanced at me. I smiled but said nothing. It took a few seconds, but she smiled back—then looked elsewhere. I turned my attention back to my computer.

I stared at the meager list of files and debated about opening my email and typing instead.

I wished I could send an email to Cami. She and Aid were the only people I would truly miss from Earth—they were pretty much the only people left to miss.

But my message would have to clear the commander before Cami could read it. And, from my experience when Ephesus had been on Mars, I knew that the commander didn't bother to approve most messages.

Ephesus said, when we were able to call him once, that he sent a message every other day.

We only ever received about ten of them.

Maybe I could start keeping a journal of my experiences. It might be worth remembering.

Then again, Mars could be just like Earth. Just a concentration camp in the sky.

"That's a cute reader."

I jerked my head up. The 20-something was looking at me again.

"Thank you. It's kind of vintage."

She smiled. It was a small smile, but a nice one. She had gray eyes—soft gray—and a sprinkling of freckles across her cheeks. "Old is sometimes better."

"Are you going to Mars?" I asked.

"Only place this transit goes," she replied.

I frowned. She was looking away again. Maybe she didn't really want to talk to me.

I looked back at my screen and opened my email. The girl spoke again.

"Is this your first time?"

"Yes."

"Moving in or traveling?"

"Father's on scientific business."

She nodded. "I live on Mars. I was just on Earth briefly." She looked at me. "What base are you going to?"

Please don't ask too many questions. "I don't remember the coordinates."

She frowned. "Do you remember the governor or anything? Who is your father working with?"

I suppose that's not a huge secret. "A governor commissioned him. Dr. Nic, I believe."

Her face lit up. "Nic! So you're with Dr. Smyrna!"

Something inside me froze. She knew who I was! How much of our status, our history, did she know? How much had she told others? Was she going to ask questions I couldn't answer—or spread gossip I didn't want repeated?

But she already knew who we were. No harm in confirming the truth.

"That's my father."

She gave me a once-over, as if this revelation changed everything. "Nic mentioned you, but I didn't realize you were coming."

"Me neither, until this morning."

She smiled widely—a somehow reassuring gesture. "It's Philadelphia, right?"

"Yeah." I paused. "But I'm usually Phil or Philli."

She nodded. "It's a pretty name. I'm Cea."

"Nice to meet you." That was the truth, I thought.

Her eyes were sparkling now. "I'm glad to meet you, too. Nic should have told me we were on the same transit—I could have come and picked you up."

I'd just as soon you didn't... I'd rather you not see the prison I came from, if you don't already know.

She must have thought my silence was begging for more explanation. "You're coming to live at my base, #9.6.11. My brother summoned you."

10

When my father came to take me to lunch and received introductions, he gave me an amazed glance—*How you do make the most convenient friends!* He later told me that he was glad I had met someone from our base who had taken a liking to me.

Cea did seem quite friendly. She stayed with me the rest of the day. In fact, I spent most of the flight with her. She ate with us at all meals, soliciting Daddy's questions about the base. She was able to tell him a little more about his situation, but she said Dr. Nic would have to fill in the technical details.

In between times, Cea and I sat apart from the crowd in the main room, sometimes with Daddy and sometimes without. We talked, mostly about base #9.6.11. She sent me to the base's promotional website—only to find that most of the pages were down.

She sighed. "Virus."

I nodded understandingly.

She decided to recite the base's history from memory instead. It was a well-known base, having been founded on experimental technology. It continued to thrive on the new and emerging and was considered a testing ground for developing theories in space settlement. The base focused on sustaining and improving life on Mars—habitat construction, air quality, gravity replication, and the like. Labs on Earth would often commission the base to test their ideas, and the world's best scientists travelled there to put their technology to work in developing new methods.

That must be what Daddy had been commissioned to do. Daddy knew he had been called because of some success in the lab, but he wasn't sure what particular area of research Dr. Nic was interested in.

The base was rather large in size but small in population. It was a rambling structure of wide wings, with more constantly being added, all used to test different theories and equipment. Cea described the place as a maze of halls connecting huge, empty—or nearly empty—rooms, where an entire wing might be devoted to seeing how long a single plant could survive in a certain set of conditions.

She smiled coyly after this description.

We didn't talk much about ourselves. Cea asked about me, and I told her the basics—how old I was, my hobbies—no, my mother was dead—that kind of thing. But when I neatly refrained from discussing details about my social status, she caught on and stopped asking.

She didn't tell me much about herself either. Just that she lived with her brother, Dr. Nic, who had been the leader of the base for nine years, taking charge at the young age of 24…

At this she launched into a proud synopsis of her brother's prodigal successes on Mars, a safe course of discussion.

Cea sat next to us when all the passengers bunkered down for landing. As soon as we were released from our seats, she led us through the crowd like she knew where she was going.

I appreciated the sense of confidence. Mars was on the other side of the transit doors.

And I had no idea what to expect.

We stepped over the threshold into the docking station, and at first I couldn't see anything except swarms of people. Cea burrowed through the crowd and pointed to a waiting room off the side of the lobby, saying, "Wait here." Daddy took my hand and pulled me out of the crowd and into the waiting room. And there, with Daddy still gripping my hand, we both had our first look at Mars.

The sun, strangely small, was slanting far in the west. I had expected the horizon to be red, but the fading light had painted the sky blue-gray like a foggy morning in London. All around, the infamous red earth was descending into black as the shadows lengthened.

I could see for what felt like a long way. A rumbling string of black lumps, with an occasional glint catching the light, blocked the northern horizon—a metropolis. Other bases dotted the land here and there like shelled beetles. There was nothing in between the bases except thick stakes topped with flashing lights—the markers dividing the land, defining the coordinates of each base.

"This is what Ephesus saw," I said aloud.

Daddy let go of my hand to put his arm around my shoulder. He rubbed my arm slightly. "He liked it. The land—it was one thing he liked about going to Mars."

Was it the only thing? I would never know.

But I would soon make my own list of what I liked—and didn't like—about living on Mars.

Someone tapped Daddy on the shoulder. We turned to see a darkly-uniformed officer armed with a gun. He coughed.

"Dr. Smyrna and daughter?"

"Yes." My father straightened.

"Your escort."

"I believe they already have an escort." Cea walked out of the crowd, frowning. "Me."

The officer glanced back at her. "Are you traveling with them?"

"I'm going the same place they are."

43

"You have your own transportation arrangements, I assume? I have been instructed to see them to their base."

"I can see them there just fine, thank you." She eyed the officer nervously.

The officer almost smiled—a condescending sort of amusement. "I'm sorry, miss, but they're unassimilated. We have regulations."

I flinched. *Regulations, regulations...*

So much for being discreet about our situation around Cea. I looked up at her.

Her eyes were wide, face white.

The officer turned back to my father. "Other baggage?"

"Yes, two checked crates."

"Claim numbers."

My father brought up the numbers on his tablet. The man held up a communicator and instructed a fellow officer to pick up our belongings.

I glanced back at Cea. She had stepped a few paces away and was mumbling into a cellphone.

The officer lowered his communicator. With a jerk of his head, he started walking.

Cea stepped in front of him. She wordlessly held out her cellphone.

The officer eyed her. Cea just wiggled the device at him.

He cautiously took it and brought it to his ear. "Hello?" Pause. "Yes, sir." Pause. "Yes, sir." The exchange was repeated half a dozen times more, then the officer sighed. He handed the phone back to Cea.

She took it and slid it into her pocket. I thought the corner of her lip twitched.

"Other arrangements have been made. I will make sure the baggage is sent to the appropriate vehicle." Then without so much as a glance at us, he walked off.

Cea grinned. "Nic said otherwise." Turning to us, she waved her arm. "You're driving over with me."

11

Our ride was a bulky little thing, like an overgrown SUV with treads. It was painted a bright blue, almost unearthly—it stood out like alien life form amongst the dull dust and glint of metal.

A generous black man was loading our crates in the back. He turned around as we approached, and his face instantly exploded into a smile.

"Smyrna, Smyrna! So good to meet... You are Dr. Smyrna, aren't you?"

"I am."

The man pumped my father's hand. "Brilliant! So glad to make your acquaintance." He nodded, as if to confirm his statement. "I'm Arnold Sardis. Meet your fellow worker." He grinned, showing all teeth.

"Pleased to meet you. Are you a scientist?" my father asked.

"No, no... Well, not your kind of science, anyway. I'm a horticulturist—plant doctor! My job is to help keep plants alive in this place. Dr. Nic would kill them all without me." He laughed pleasantly.

He glanced down and spotted me. "Now, who's this?" He bent over to be more at my eye-level, planting his hands on his large knees.

"Philadelphia, sir," I replied politely.

"Oh? You must be the daughter! I didn't realize you were coming."

Most people weren't, it seems...

"Delightful news! So glad to have both of you." He grabbed my arm with both hands and shook it gleefully.

"We'd best be going," Cea said, taking my carry-on and dropping it in the trunk.

"Of course, of course. Come now, load up." Mr. Sardis sauntered over to the driver's seat and climbed in.

Cea closed the trunk and sat next to him. Daddy and I shared the middle, buckling into the sturdy and well-cushioned seats.

Mr. Sardis joined the lines of vehicles waiting to exit. We drove into a tunnel, where the gate behind us closed before the one in front of us opened. Our SUV rumbled down a ramp, and we were out in the open.

It was a relatively smooth ride—and a quiet one, with the engine gurgling lowly. I watched the multicolored ground pass beneath the treads.

The area around the docking bay was thickly inhabited by bases. Mr. Sardis wove around the bubbles and blocks, ducking under bridges that connected some of the metal homes. After a half-hour, however, the bases thinned, until there were only one or two dotting the horizon.

Another half-hour, and then we passed through a section of country where there were no bases at all—none. Endless red, quickly turning into the color of dried blood as the sun faded. Only the regular stakes, every kilometer, divided the sea in a rigid grid pattern.

Slowly, it rose on the horizon. At first, it looked like a tiny bug; as we drew closer, it seemed to grow before our eyes, sending out legs and multiplying. Rambling, glass glinting in the last shot of sunlight—it was base #9.6.11.

A wide hall with a curved glass roof ran down the center. The lower half of the base was fairly narrow, but the structure widened rapidly towards the north end. Wing built upon wing, sprawling out across the land—some rooms stuck out in the middle of nowhere, connected to the rest of the base by a snaking hallway. Some had windows, some had not; some were above ground, some half below. Dozens of shades—but all made out of metal.

At the far southern end, a docking bay bulged out. The gates opened to welcome us, and the SUV chugged up the ramp. The gate closed; there was a brief pause before a panel on the wall glowed green. Great doors slid open, letting in a flood of light from the rest of the base, and we all got out.

Someone stood in the hallway, beckoning to us. I couldn't see his face—the lights behind him were so much brighter than the ambiance in the bay. I shielded my eyes as Daddy took my hand and led me in.

"Dr. Smyrna!" It was a diplomatic voice, but not an unkind one. "You have made it at last."

I blinked, vision adjusting. Father let go of my hand to shake that of a man younger than himself.

He was only in his mid-30s, with a sophisticated little mustache under his nose. He had dusty blond hair like Cea, only his was straight and primly styled. His eyes were like Cea's too, only darker—almost bluish gray.

He smiled—again, a business-like smile, but a genuine one. "Dr. Nic, Governor," he explained.

"Honored to make your acquaintance," my father replied.

Dr. Nic's eyes sparkled. "The same, and more so. I've been awaiting your arrival. Your expertise is extremely coveted here."

"I appreciate the commission."

More so, 'I appreciate your allowing my daughter to accompany me...'

Dr. Nic glanced down at me. "So this is the daughter! What was your name again?"

"Philadelphia." I bobbed. It felt appropriate.

He liked it. He smiled. "You are welcome here."

That must have been the truth. Perhaps he had been the one to arrange my passage.

"I'm sure you're eager to see the base…"

"I'm sure you're eager to show it off," Cea quipped.

Dr. Nic rubbed his mustache. "So you met my sister, I hear."

"Phil found me." Cea shrugged.

"Did she? How convenient we have you along, then, Phil." He laughed. "Yes, I am eager to be the proud parent of my little kingdom. But! Some things must wait until morning. I'll show you to your rooms—rest well, please. Work must start immediately in the morning. No time to waste!"

He started walking. We followed. "Sardis, can you transfer the baggage?"

"I got it, I got it!"

We exited the receiving room and walked out into the main hall. Strips of lights glowed along the wall, and the glass-domed ceiling showed the darkening sky above. The hall stretched on, straight ahead, as far as I could see. All along the tunnel were doors, marked with numbers and letters above. Each door had a digital panel to the side.

Everything was made out of metal. Metal on the floor, metal on the ceiling, metal in the doors and the frames around the glass.

Dr. Nic walked a short distance up the main hall and turned off to the left. The big doors, marked with a number 5, opened automatically. Inside there was a foyer dotted with plants and two benches. Beneath the glass ceiling were two levels of smaller doors, marked with letters. There were six doors on each level, spaced erratically.

"F will be your quarters." Dr. Nic gestured to the door on the lower level, far right. "Let me set the lock."

He walked up to the darkened panel at the side of the door. He reached into his pocket and pulled out a chubby disc decorated with buttons. He held it close to the panel, and it snapped into place.

He pressed a button, and the door slid open with a beep. He removed the disc and gestured to my father and me. "Hold your hands over the panel. No need to touch it—just stretch your fingers out like that. One at a time, or it might mess the system up."

Father went first. A moment of orange, then a happy green circle flashed across the display. Dr. Nic nodded at me.

I slowly extended my fingers and held them over the black screen. The orange dash contemplated, then chirped. The green circle blinked, as if saying, *Welcome home, new resident!*

After a few seconds of silence, the door beeped again and slid shut. "The doors will open only for you now when they're locked," Dr. Nic explained. "There's instructions on the other side on how to lock it and all that."

My father tested the apparatus. He waved his hand over the sensor. The green circle appeared, and the doors reopened.

"No thumbprint scan?" he questioned.

"The panel is designed to scan DNA through the hand. Much more reliable than a face scan, more sanitary than a thumbprint. Just one of the many innovations we're pioneering up here." Dr. Nic smiled. "Well, go on then."

I followed Dad into the apartment. Inside was a cozy sitting room. Beyond, three doors—two on the right, and one in the back.

"Two bedrooms and a washroom. Should be sufficient. Let me know if you find the accommodations unsuitable," Dr. Nic said honestly.

My father walked into the middle of the room, gazing around at the smooth walls and flat ceiling. "No... no, they'll be just fine."

I cautiously approached his side.

Mr. Sardis came in, followed by an older, slender fellow. He was so pale, with gray hair and a white coat, that he looked like a piece of blank paper next to Mr. Sardis. They deposited our crates in the middle of the floor.

"Carnegie, my assistant," Dr. Nic gestured at the elderly man.

Carnegie took us in with his green eyes, as if measuring our competency. He nodded and left without a word. Mr. Sardis waved, smiled, and left right behind him.

Dr. Nic walked towards the door. "One of us will be along to collect you at 9, Doctor, and orient you."

Cea stood in the doorway to the hall. "I'll come get you about 9:30, Phil, and show you around."

Dr. Nic stopped and regarded his sister. "Excellent idea." His diplomatic smile returned.

He glanced back at us. "Welcome to Mars." He flicked his hand over the sensor and stood there smiling while the door closed. Cea watched from behind him.

Finally alone, I looked around the room. Neatly furnished, it looked cozier than our home on Earth. It was certainly artsier—a large digital frame on the wall scrolled through stunning images of the galaxy, while a few potted plants broke up the monotony of metal and plastic. Unlike the rest of the halls, a gray carpet softened the floor.

Daddy touched my shoulder.

"Was Ephesus's room like this?" I asked.

"I imagine so." He paused. "But now it's ours. Our home, Phil."

Home. Home was metal. So much metal.

But then again, on Earth I had been surrounded by concrete. I didn't suppose metal was much different.

I could only pray that metal would be more tolerant of Christians.

Cea

12

Before Daddy left in the morning, he told me to listen to Cea, to not get in anybody's way, and to generally behave. Mr. Sardis came to pick Daddy up—our hallway door was open, and we heard his whistling long before we saw him. He swaggered into the room, calling out boisterous greetings.

He had a little potted plant cupped in his hands—his skin was almost the same color as the rich dirt. He presented the tiny red blooms to me and said I ought to have a little color for my room.

Daddy smiled on while I thanked him.

I closed and locked the door after they left. While I waited for Cea, I sat on the couch and studied the sheet of instructions for the door so I would know how to get back in later.

Like Dr. Nic had said, the door worked by scanning DNA through the fingertips, making it easy to control access. There was an identical panel on the inside and outside of each door, and the sensors could be set from either side. Only Dr. Nic knew how to reset the system once the door had been programmed. When the door was locked, it would only open for the approved sets of

DNA. When Cea came, I would have to open the door from the inside for her.

That made me wonder how Cea would announce her presence when she came. Would she knock—or was there a doorbell? Could I hear her through the metal door if she called? What would I do all day after Cea showed me around? Would it be easy to stay out of everyone's way? Most of the residents were scientists—were they set up to accommodate families, or was I the only tagalong? After all, my attendance had been an impromptu decision.

"Phil?"

I jumped when Cea called me—and so clear! Her voice was loud, though slightly electronic. I scanned the room as I got up and unlocked the door.

"Where is your voice coming from?" I asked as she came in.

"My mouth?"

"No, I mean, when the door's closed. I can hear you so clearly. Where..."

"Oh, there's a speaker at most doors." She gestured to the control panel mounted by the doorframe. "So you can contact those inside. Otherwise nobody would be able to hear anything around here. Just press the button marked 'call.'"

"Clever," I said, feeling anything but.

"If you want to talk back without opening the door, hit this orange button from the inside. It opens the communication two-way." She smiled. "Ready for breakfast?"

We didn't head straight to breakfast. Cea took me on a tour of the base between the docking bay and the cafeteria. She didn't take me down any halls, just showed me the gates and told me what was beyond—after she told me how to distinguish a gate from any other kind of door.

Gates were taller and marked with only numbers—1, 4, 23. Anything beyond a gate was a wing. Everything through Gate 19 was considered Wing 19, until you got to another gate, and so on. Within gates, doors were marked with letters and the wing number—1C, 4A, 23D. Some doors would open to halls with more doors, which would be marked with letters followed by decimals—1C.2, 4A.6, 23D.9.

I didn't ask what happened if you opened a door in a hall which led to another hall.

What I wanted to do was ask her was to repeat everything two or three more times. I felt lost just standing still in the middle of the main hallway. Was the system nonsensical, or was I simply too stupid to grasp it?

Maybe a little bit of both.

Thankfully, most of the halls at the southern end of the base were straightforward. The docking bay was marked simply DOCK. Agreeable. Cea told me that the main hall, with the glass dome ceiling, was considered Wing 1. If the call number of any room was preceded by a 1, it was off the main hall. We passed 1A, which was a meeting room, and 1B, which was an auditorium. Gate 2 lead to offices and general rooms, as did Gate 3 opposite. Gate 4 and 5, across from each other, were the main cabins.

I noticed that, so far, all the odd-numbered gates were on the left. I wondered if that was consistent throughout the base.

Probably not.

Just past the cabins were Gate 6, which led to a medical and sickbay, and Gate 7. Cea led me through the latter—the door opened automatically—and I smelled bread and heard running water.

The main cafeteria was straight ahead. The floor and walls were bright white, a sort of plastic instead of metal. The rounded glass ceiling let in streams of brilliant light, making the place almost blinding. The room was scattered with tables of various sizes, interspersed with plants. There were a few doors along the back wall—Cea said they were private dining rooms—and access to the kitchen, with a long buffet, was to the right.

The place was almost deserted already. Two white-coated scientists nodded at us as they left. A businessman lounged by himself in the back corner, chattering into his cellphone in what sounded like Mandarin. In the middle of the room, a dark-skinned woman was wiping the face of a chubby toddler. Both looked up and smiled at me, the toddler waving jam-covered fingers.

I waved back. Perhaps my father wasn't the only scientist who brought his family with him.

While we ate our selections from the healthful buffet, Cea ran down a loose schedule. I would normally eat breakfast and lunch by myself. I hoped that Daddy would sometimes be able to eat with me, but that would depend on his workload. Dinner, Cea said, was up to my father and me—but, in general, the scientists usually worked from 9:00-19:00.

Curfew was at midnight, unless one had a special pass. The base's systems, except for the dorms, went into hibernation mode from midnight until 5 to save power and allow for repairs. That's also when the base's clocks collectively rolled back 40 minutes to account for Mars' slightly longer rotation.

"Nic decided it was just easier this way," Cea explained with a wry grin. "So far, no one's complained about getting an extra 40 minutes of sleep every day."

Little else on base ran on an official schedule. Everyone plotted out the workday for themselves, depending on what project they were assigned to.

I wondered what I would find to fill my days.

As we were walking back to the dorms, Cea suggested an activity for the morning. "Want help unpacking?"

I thought of the crate waiting patiently on my bedroom floor. "Sure—thank you. Though, there isn't much."

I didn't want to think about the fact that I wouldn't have had *any* luggage had I not been packed to go to the Nolans'.

I let us back into my room. Cea glanced sideways at me. "Did you not bring most of your stuff?"

Oh, I brought it all... everything that didn't stay with the house because it belonged to the government...

"Or did you not have that much to bring?"

I looked away.

"I'm sorry..." Her voice reached out to me. "That was harsh. I was just wondering... if it's really like they say."

I looked back at her. "They who?"

"They... about Earth. About... the unassimilated concentration camps." She stared into my face, eyes wide and revealing. "Is it really... bad?"

"These are all the belongings I have. Everything else either belonged to the camp or was the school's." I took the lid off the metal crate and pulled out a stack of clothes.

Cea bent and took out a few shirts. "I've heard rumors... but most of the people here, they don't know. They don't care. 'That's Earth's business.' But I was curious... You don't have to talk about it if you don't want to."

"So you know?" I hit the button to open the mirrored closet doors.

"About?"

"About us... being Christians. That... we're not here of our own free will." I stared into the dark closet. Then I flipped on the light and spoke my mind. "Slaves."

"Don't you want to be here?" She followed me into the closet.

"Yes!" The exclamation was out of my mouth before I had time to think it—but I felt it.

"I knew," she responded. "Nic talked about having to go through the commander... Ambrose, is that his name?"

I nodded as I clipped a skirt on a hanger. "Does everyone else know?"

"I'm not sure... Why would they care?"

I didn't answer. I held the hanger up and let it snap onto the magnetic rod. *The same reason people on Earth care.*

I took the shirts from her. She walked back to the crate and changed the subject. "Where did you go to school?"

"Same high school as everyone else. We just had extra 'remedial' classes."

"Oh."

"They started making us go about five years ago. We homeschooled before that." I started hanging up shirts. "Speaking of school, I'm not sure if I should finish and get my diploma, or maybe take some higher-level courses... I was thinking some school might be a nice way to keep me occupied, out of trouble, you know?"

Cea was silent. I glanced over at her. She was bent over the crate, holding our digital picture frame in her hands.

The picture of Ephesus was still on the screen.

Cea frowned and squinted.

"That's my older brother," I explained.

She jerked her head up. Her face was colorless. "He's your brother?"

"Was." I looked down at the gray sweater in my hands. "He was sent to Mars on scientific business as well... But his transit home exploded."

"I know," Cea said quietly. She groaned and pinched the bridge of her nose. "Nic, you—" The next word she used was definitely not a term of endearment.

I stepped towards her. "What's the matter?" When she didn't answer right away, I abandoned the question in lieu of one that seemed more pertinent: "You knew my brother?"

She nodded and stood up. She held the frame close to the wall, and the magnets snapped into place. "I've met him." She gave the corner a tweak, adjusting the position. She regarded the image for a moment, then glanced back at me.

"This was the base he worked at."

13

No one said anything for a long time.

I stared, but not at Cea. I stared out my bedroom window at the dusty ground, the desert, the red—the view my brother saw.

"I'm sorry," Cea said at last. She let out a sigh and whispered again, "I'm sorry."

"Was this... was this his room? Did he... did he sleep in these cabins?" I walked into the middle of the floor, footsteps muted on the carpet—was that the sound my brother heard? Did he stand at that window, hang his coat in that closet?

"No. He slept in some dorms closer to the wing he was working in. It was a commissioned test... Well, I'm sure he told you about it."

I shook my head. "Only vaguely. He didn't know going in what his assignment was... and he... he wasn't able to write much."

"He wrote you all the time," she said incredulously. "Every other day, he'd turn in a half-hour early, saying he was writing home."

My mind spun with images of my brother, waving off fellow scientists, walking back to his room with a purposed air... in front of a computer, in the dark, typing furiously... only to pause, and blink...

"Didn't he tell you anything about his work?"

"He probably did. But we didn't get most of the messages."

She tipped her head to the side. I looked away, but I didn't see any reason not to tell her the truth.

"The commander has to approve all incoming and outgoing messages. Most of them, he doesn't."

Cea was silent. Her tone changed. "Do you... want to see his rooms?"

*

"Your brother's dorm was way back in Wing 88, right outside Wing 89."

We walked quickly down the hall. I listened to Cea's voice, but my eyes scanned the gates and doors as we passed, trying to grasp the numbers—12, 12C, 14... I had only gotten a tour up to Wing 7, and we'd left that behind a long time ago. We'd turned off the main hall into Wing 12, then through Wing 14, which jumped to Wing 27...

"89 was where his assignment was, and they were going nearly 'round the clock for a while. It was just easier to sleep over there. Or at least that was Nic's logic."

Cea shrugged. She waved her hand over the sensor for Gate 30 and waited for it to open.

"I guess it was that important. It was *the* test that year. Big dollars, famous scientists. Your brother was among them."

I'd never thought of my brother as "famous." How famous can an unassimilated get in the United? He had been wanted in the lab ever since he'd graduated from college—long hours, some months rarely home. Maybe that makes you "famous" in the science world, especially when you're so young.

all, Nic called him up here just for that test."

Daddy. Was Daddy "famous" too?

we passed into the 40s. Through one hall, into the 50s... And there was Gate 88. Where were the 60s? 70s? Was there no logic to the numbers?

No logic from Earth, that was sure.

We passed through Gate 88 into a wing that was completely silent. We hadn't seen another human being for a while, but there was a different kind of stillness about this hall. All the doors were shut, keypads dark. The main hall was dimly lit with muted security lights instead of the brilliant beams of the rest of the base. The tunnel ended in blackness, as though it snaked on into nothingness and ceased to exist.

Cea walked down to the third door on the left and opened it. Then she stepped back and gestured at me.

I didn't hesitate. Why, I don't know—I felt like stalling, like avoiding it, like waiting a few more minutes. But my feet strode up to the doorway and stopped.

I looked in—and something in me died.

There was nothing in there. The lights were dark. The bed was stripped. Nothing was on the walls, the desk, the nightstand. Nothing. It was bare metal, a shell.

There were no pieces of my brother left. Nothing—nothing personal. It was as though he had never been there.

And for as much as I could get at him, he might as well have never been here.

"Not much, I suppose, but I thought you'd like to see it anyway. Poor substitute for his emails, though. I'm sure he described it to you in one of his notes."

"Why is it... empty?"

"Because no one's living in there anymore."

"But..." I turned around and pointed towards the end of the hall. "Why so... dark. So... unused?"

Cea followed my gaze. "Wing 89 is closed. The test is done."

"Why haven't they reused it?"

"The test failed. Badly. Some chemicals they were using… they think that's what caused the transit to explode." She looked into my face. "It didn't look good, for the science."

I stared into the blackness. Cea closed the door and started to walk back towards the gate.

I followed. "What happened… to his things?"

"What things?"

"Ephesus's things. His belongings. Where are they now?" I thought of the completely bare surfaces in the room.

She squinted. "I don't… know."

"They must have done something with them after he died. Did they save them? Are they still here somewhere?"

Cea shook her head faintly. Suddenly, she straightened, and realization hit her eyes. "Weren't they on the transit with him?"

My silence said everything. Somehow, I managed to keep walking.

We wove through a few halls before Cea spoke again. Her voice sounded far away, as though she were on the other side of a wall. "I'm sorry."

I watched the marked doors shift past. "I had no reason to expect anything. He's gone. All of him."

I paused. Why was I sharing my life's woes with Cea? Then again, what harm would it do to tell her? She had known Ephesus; she might—just maybe—even care.

"Being here… won't make him feel any closer. He's as far away as he's always been."

Unreachable. Always was, always will be, this side of heaven. He'd been dead ever since he left Earth.

Being here might just make it hurt even worse.

Cea walked a few steps ahead of me and held her hand over the sensor for a gate. It opened, and Dr. Nic appeared in the doorway like a picture in a frame.

"Well, I didn't even have to touch the sensor!"

"Oh, hi Nic."

He smiled that politically correct smile. He looked at his sister, who stared back—after a moment, she smiled. I thought I saw a bit of understanding, a flicker of sibling sympathy, pass between them.

It broke when Dr. Nic noticed me. "I was looking for you... Well, you have a buddy today! Making friends quickly, I see, sister?"

"Phil's a natural." Cea shrugged and stuffed her hands in her pockets.

Dr. Nic laughed. "Stop that. I'm glad, and you know it." Cea didn't respond, so he looked at me. "And what, might I ask, are you two girls doing?"

"She's showing me my—"

Cea spoke at the same time. "I'm just giving her the tour."

Dr. Nic nodded. "And how does our new colonist like the establishment?"

I blinked. "I've hardly had time to absorb it all."

"I'll take that as a good sign." He grinned, then coughed. "Well, Cea, I've been looking for you. I need you for a bit, if your buddy can spare you."

"I'll go find my father," I offered, hoping to be helpful.

Dr. Nic smiled approvingly. "He's on break. See you at dinner, Phil." He walked past me and opened another gate.

Cea trotted to match pace with him. "I'll catch you later!"

"Bye," I said, and watched the door close behind them.

It was only after the gate sealed shut that it occurred to me that going to find my father was easier said than done.

I looked up at the gate in front of me: Gate 69.

Wait a second. Hadn't we skipped the 60s on the way here? Had Cea taken a different route back?

I sighed, then shook my head. Surely there were multiple ways to get back to Wing 1. As long as I moved in the right direction, I'd eventually get there. In theory.

Straightening my shoulders, I opened Gate 69 and continued through. There was only one way to find out.

14

About an hour later, I had my answer.

I was lost. Utterly.

I hadn't seen a familiar gate number in at least half an hour. Sometimes I would find myself in the low numbers, and I felt like I was getting close—and then the next gate I would pass through would dump me back into the 80s. Once I even passed through a segment of the 90s.

It was as if I were going in circles, which was a reasonable assumption.

I sighed. What irked me most was the fact that I had not managed to pass another human being in all this time. Very few of the halls I had walked through contained anything more than doors.

I entered a wing with several gates and walked up to the closest one. At this point, it didn't really matter which one I tried.

I waved my hand over the sensor, and the panel released the most hideous sound I had ever heard. I almost screamed out of shock.

I dared to look down at the panel. An ugly red X glowed, with the words *Access Denied* flashing below it.

I stared at the words until the red faded away. Access denied?

The door wasn't set to accept me. Which meant I was most assuredly going in the wrong direction.

I moaned and tried another gate. Also locked. The next three ones I tried were locked as well. That sound was really starting to get on my nerves.

I cringed as I held my hand over the next gate, waiting for the beep. It didn't. It flashed green and opened agreeably.

I pushed loose hairs off my forehead and walked through, hoping for the best. The sight beyond made me stop and stare.

It was the strangest wing I had been in yet. It was massive—the size of a warehouse—but completely bare. There were only three gates in the entire place.

Two were on my side of the room—Gate 72, and Gate 73, which I had just come out of. Across the room was Gate 74.

I figured I might as well try the one across the room. Gate 72 probably led back the way I came, though there was no guarantee of that.

I held my breath while I tried the door. I let it out when the panel accepted me readily.

I walked through and immediately wondered if Gate 72 would have been a safer bet. The lights in Wing 74 were dim—had I run into another unused wing?

I shrugged. I was here. I might as well give it a go.

Wing 74 was lined with doors. I walked up to the first and tried it. *Access Denied.* Second and third doors were the same. After the fifth refusal, I began to worry.

I glanced around the hall and noticed something peculiar about the gates. They were unmarked. No numbers, no letters. Just bare doors.

Bare doors that, honestly, looked like nobody had been through them in years. Dust and debris gathered in the corners, and several of the access panels still had protective film on the screen. If it weren't for the fact that the middle of the hall was swept clean, I would have thought the wing hadn't been used in a decade.

I suddenly felt the urge to speak aloud. It was just too creepy being in a hall of unmarked doors without evidence of a single soul.

"All these halls!" was the only thing I could think of to say.

My voice reverberated off the metal, and I instantly regretted speaking. The echo was surreal. I glanced back over my shoulder and waited until the silence returned. This time, it was welcome.

I drew in a deep breath and kept walking. If I got in here, I could get out. At the very least, if I didn't find a door that opened, I would go back out of Gate 74.

Yes. A reasonable plan.

I continued down the hall. The ambiance of the lighting began to unnerve me; moving constantly in and out of shadow was disturbing. I tried more unmarked doors, all locked. A few at least looked like they had been used recently, but they still didn't let me in. Just as I was beginning to wonder if I'd reached the point where I'd better turn back, a door opened for me.

I almost shrieked in relief. After all the red X's, the green circle was the most comforting thing I'd ever seen.

I passed through the door—and found myself in that empty wing again. I frowned and glanced back at the door.

Gate 74. Again.

I sighed. Well, at least I was out. And I knew which way *not* to go.

I went back through the gate I had come in by—at least, I hoped it was the same gate. I found myself in a wing with several more gates, and I picked the smallest number. Maybe if I kept doing that, I would eventually end up at Wing 1.

The door opened before I could touch the panel, and I almost screamed for the third time in an hour. Then I promptly wanted to collapse in relief—Dr. Nic and Cea were standing on the other side of the door.

It felt cheap, but I had to say it: "I am so glad you're here! I—"

"What are you doing back here?" Dr. Nic's voice was more of a snarl than a question.

"Lost," I confessed readily. "You left me, and I tried to get back to Wing 1, and I—"

"You should not be back here," he interrupted me again. Cea glanced between us.

"Don't I know it." I sighed, then looked up pathetically. "I don't suppose you know the way back?"

Cea stepped up and took charge. "Of course. I'm sorry, Phil, I shouldn't have left you alone. I should have given you directions or something. It's my fault." She glanced sideways at her brother.

Dr. Nic's scowl melted into his diplomatic smile. He actually laughed. "Of course! I should have thought of that. Just stay with Cea and don't go wandering around. It's not safe."

Cea abruptly started walking. I called over my shoulder as I ran to keep up with her. "I won't, I promise!"

His smile faded. "Good." He stood still and watched us until the gate closed.

15

I had to run to keep pace with Cea. She didn't slow down until we were back in the 30s.

"I'm sorry, Cea, I didn't mean to make trouble."

Cea abruptly reduced her pace to a casual walk, as if she suddenly realized she was running. I almost bumped into her. "It's okay." She let out her breath, and her voice returned to normal. "You didn't mean it."

"I didn't mess anything up, I don't think." I struggled to steady my breathing after the sprint. "I didn't see any rooms with equipment or people, so I'm pretty sure I didn't disturb anything."

"Where did you go?" Cea opened a door, and there was Wing 1. I was so glad to see the sky shimmering above the glass dome.

"Everywhere and nowhere. I passed so many numbers that I don't remember any at all—except Wing 74. That was weird."

"What?" Cea stopped and looked at me. "Where?"

I thought, making sure I had my numbers correct. "Wing 74. It was way in the back. Well, it felt like it was way in the back. It was weird, because all the doors weren't marked."

"Unmarked doors…?" She squinted. "I'm not aware of a hall with unmarked doors. Are you sure?"

I nodded. "Positive."

Cea's face was set in a disturbing frown. "Let's go check." She started walking again.

"Go check?" I repeated.

Cea walked a few paces down the hall and opened the door for Room 1C. She ushered me inside and locked the door behind us.

The room was almost completely bare. There were a few chairs inside the door and a computer terminal in the back corner. The walls were blank and windowless. A section of the ceiling in the far right corner was dotted with black sensor eyes.

I pointed. "What's that on the ceiling?"

"You'll see." Cea walked over to the terminal and waved her hand in front of the screen. A menu appeared. "Do you remember what time it was when I left you?"

I struggled to remember the last time I had touched base with a clock. "It was about an hour ago, I think."

Cea typed on the keypad. There was the faint sound of static, and suddenly a holographic copy of me was standing in the room!

Cea laughed when I jumped. "Sorry, I should have warned you. It's the security tape. Watch."

I did. It was a ghostly version of me—faded and slightly transparent. But the colors were correct, and I moved as though real. The sound was real. I listened as my footsteps and my ghost walked towards the far corner of the room. Gate 69 could be seen behind me.

My ghost walked off the edge of the projection. Cea touched the computer screen, and the background shifted to the next camera's viewpoint. My replica walked into view again, stepping out of thin air on the edge of the image. The hologram formed under the square of black-dotted ceiling; when my ghost reached the edge of the sensors, it vanished.

Cea switched viewpoints again. She tucked a curl of hair behind her ear and rapidly pawed through menus. "It's hard to track a moving body, because you have to keep switching cameras, but it works."

We traced my ghost as it wandered the maze, twisting through random doors. I felt lost again.

"You were going in the right direction up until this point. This is where you took a wrong turn." Cea walked into the hologram and pointed at a door marked Gate 45. "You should have gone here."

"Oh," I said as my replica took Gate 43 on the other side of the room.

Cea backed out of the hologram and stood beside me. We watched my image try random doors, cringing at the horrible beep of denial.

Cea frowned. "You got way out of course, girl. There's nothing down that hall."

"Nothing for me, anyway! None of the doors would let me in."

"Why did you keep trying them?" She walked back to the terminal.

"Um… I figured the doors closer to Wing 1 were set to accept me. So if the door opened, I was going in the right direction."

I hoped Cea would laugh at my incompetence. Not surprisingly, she didn't.

I jumped and pointed. "There it is! Gate 74. That's the gate that leads to a hall with unmarked doors… and none of them would open."

My ghost walked up to Gate 74. Cea straightened. Her eyes narrowed. My hologram waved its hand, then sighed with relief as the panel flashed green. It walked into the hall and disappeared out of range.

The image abruptly went blank. I glanced back at Cea. She rapidly tapped the screen. "You walked out of range of our security cameras."

"But there were more halls beyond Gate 74... lots of them! None of the doors would open, and none of them were marked."

"How did you get out?" Cea's eyes were wide.

I shrugged. "I made a big circle... When I finally found a door that would open, it was Gate 74 again."

Cea shook her head and turned back to the terminal. "I don't know where you went, Phil."

"Why are there no cameras beyond Gate 74?"

"I've never been back there... maybe it's unused." She paused. "Or unfinished. Since the doors aren't marked or anything."

I remembered the dusty corners around the doors. Maybe it was construction debris.

Cea shrugged. "I'll have to ask Nic—I don't know." She went back to scrolling. "I wouldn't worry about it. You won't have to go back there again—there's nothing back there."

She continued typing. I regarded the bare room, the empty stage. Slowly, "Cea... are all the security records on that computer?"

"Most of them," she replied. "Anything that's public."

"How far... do they go back?"

"Since the cameras were put in." The terminal beeped at her.

"Are there... any records from when..." I stopped.

She looked up at me. "From what?"

"Ephesus?" I whispered. I turned to face her. "Do you have any records from when Ephesus was here?"

She regarded me. Compassion flickered across her gray eyes. "Yes."

"Can... you?"

"Do you want to see them?" she asked.

I looked down at the floor and battled. "Yes, I do."

Without a word, Cea turned and touched the screen. She thumbed through several menus, then dropped her arm. I waited.

The image snapped into place, but at first I couldn't see anyone. It was a meeting room somewhere, with a vacant table in the middle. I bit my lip.

Voices echoed somewhere off the recording. I heard him, jumbled amongst other men. I tensed my nerves as he walked into view.

There he was, perpetual lab coat and all. He walked to the table and leaned on his knuckles. The other men gathered around. One laid a tablet on the table, and they began discussing the chart displayed on it.

I had no idea what Ephesus was saying. I couldn't grasp the words—technical gibberish—but I didn't care. All I wanted was his voice.

It matched the memories in my head perfectly. Some secret fear in me died.

I took a step towards him. I took another step—I was standing right beside him. He felt real. Thin but real. I reached out my finger to tap his arm.

My hand went right through.

I cupped my palm and brought back air. I stared at my fingers, as though hoping something would materialize on them.

I looked back up at Ephesus. The tears in my eyes made his image blur.

"Do you want me to shut it off?" Cea asked carefully.

I backed out of the hologram. "No... no."

We both watched in silence as the men finished their meeting. Ephesus left, and the recording continued to display a blank room. Cea shut the hologram off.

"You can look through the files," she said, walking away from the computer. "You can watch whatever's on file. If it's on that computer, it's public."

I took her place before the terminal. "Do you have... the day he died?"

"Some. A couple of the records were removed to investigate the accident. But... I wouldn't recommend watching that day."

I drew a breath and nodded. The computer screen displayed a form field and a "browse" button.

"If you know what you're looking for, enter the specs and it will pull up the exact recording. But you have to know which camera you want."

I shook my head and hit "browse," then "search by date."

Cea walked away. She paused in the doorway. "Phil... be careful."

I looked up at her. "Thank you."

She stared back at me. Then she left.

I entered 2073 into the year field, then August. I wanted to see when Ephesus arrived on base for the first time. What day was it?

Something in the corner of the screen caught my eye: "History."

I opened the menu. The most recent entry was dated 2074—the meeting. The entry before it was for this morning, not long ago.

I tapped it. I wanted to see Gate 74 again.

The computer screeched, a sound akin to *Access Denied*. I swallowed.

A red-bordered message appeared on the screen. I blinked to make sure it was real.

Error: File not found.

16

After two hours, I was miserable.

I thought looking at recordings of Ephesus would ease the pain by filling the gap in my memory, allowing me to relive time we had been separated.

Instead, they tore the bandage off an old wound by reminding me that I had missed, been completely left out of, the last days of my brother's life.

Most of the recordings were mundane, of him in meetings, or walking down the hall, or toying with some scientific gadgetry. Those didn't bother me.

The ones that hit me were the few rare recordings that caught him reclining in a lounge, or sitting by himself in the cafeteria—of him being relaxed. Because whenever he was relaxed, whenever he could not distract his mind with work, I saw the oft-buried emotion surface in his eyes. I could see the brotherliness, the confusion, the loneliness, the thoughtfulness. The pain.

It was then that I could tell he had missed me just as much as I'd missed him.

Once, the tape caught him reading his Bible during lunch. The highlighted text filled the screen of his laptop while he added yet another note to the overflowing sidebar. I had once sat beside him on the couch while he wrote those notes.

That was when I turned the recording off and cried.

I didn't feel like eating lunch after that. I sat in our dorms and prayed, wondering if Daddy would come anytime soon.

He didn't, but Cea did.

"Phil?"

I briefly glanced at the monitor, wondering if I wanted to employ the two-way communication feature. I decided against it and let her in.

"You weren't at lunch and I..." She trailed off.

I turned away to face the digital picture frame. "I'm all right," I answered her question before she could ask it. "Physically."

"Ephesus?"

"Yes."

"I'm sorry."

"You warned me." I let out my breath.

She was silent for a moment. "You should go eat something. They're still serving lunch for another half-hour."

"Okay," I said in ambiguous consent.

I expected the cafeteria to be empty, but it wasn't. Mr. Sardis occupied a table with the woman and toddler I'd seen at breakfast—presumably his wife and son. They were laughing and playing with the boy, copying his silly noises.

I scooped up a little food and sat on the opposite side of the room. I was glad Cea hadn't insisted on sitting with me.

I stirred my food for at least three minutes before eating any of it, turning my selections into one homogenous mush. I didn't even notice the horrible taste, probably because my mind was still choking on grief over Ephesus.

The image of him highlighting a verse in his digital Bible repeatedly came back to me. I wanted to know what he had been reading. I wanted to know what he had highlighted—what verse had struck him and encouraged him. Because I needed that same touch.

I needed that Bible.

But his computer was reduced to ashes, scattered on the four winds of empty space, along with him and the entire transit. If only his scheduled flight had been one transit sooner, or if only his baggage had gotten put on the wrong transit…

It hit me so hard I nearly gagged on my obliterated potatoes.

His baggage hadn't been on the transit with him. Or, at least, not all of it.

He was only coming back for a visit. Not specifically to visit us, of course—the United wasn't that kind—but to do some research-whatever in the lab. He should only have taken enough baggage to last him a week.

Granted, my brother didn't have that many belongings. He probably took most of his clothes.

Would he have left his computer behind? If he did, would it have the Bible on it? He probably took his personal laptop, but he had more than one computer for work. He'd copied the Bible to his personal laptop before leaving, I remembered that. Maybe he transferred the file to his other work laptops, too. He had an encrypted app on his phone; it wouldn't surprise me if he'd put a copy of the file on all his devices.

And if he did, that laptop might be shut off, tucked away in storage somewhere, safe from the virus. With a Bible resting on its hard drive.

It was a stretch. If the computers were for work, the lab probably took them back. But the rest of his goods, whatever wasn't on the transit, had to be somewhere.

And at this point, I would do anything to get my hands on even the tiniest piece of him.

A scraping chair broke my reverie. Mrs. Sardis and her son were leaving. She smiled as she passed my table; the little boy waved.

"Hi," he called.

"Hi!" I replied. The happy tone of my voice was genuine.

I stood up. Mr. Sardis still sat alone, munching on his dessert. Maybe he would know.

I walked over to his table. He turned, grinned, and swallowed his mouthful.

"Hello again, Philli!" he burst out. He sure picked up on my nickname quickly. "Enjoying yourself?"

"Yes," I said, which may or may not have been the truth. "I have a question."

"Fantastic! I might know the answer." He winked and took another bite.

I searched for a way to clearly phrase my question. "If I were looking for some baggage, where would it be?"

"Did I forget some of your luggage?" He licked frosting off his lips and looked properly horrified.

"No..." I chewed my jaw. How much did I want to explain? Did it really matter? If Cea knew about Ephesus, Mr. Sardis probably did too.

"I'm looking for some baggage my brother left behind."

"You've got a brother? You really need to be more open about your family relationships. First a surprise daughter, now you're telling me you have a brother!"

I sighed. Might as well take the plunge. "Ephesus Smyrna. He worked here a few years ago. The... transit exploded."

The smile died from his eyes, and his big voice dropped to a tiny whisper. "Oh."

"Do you know where they put his stuff?" I asked hopefully.

He scrunched his face. "What stuff? Didn't he have all his baggage with him?"

"No!" I protested, a little too loudly. "He was just coming back for a visit. He should have left some things behind. Where would they have put it?"

"I... don't know." He abruptly leaned back and ran a hand through his hair. After a second, he straightened and looked at me carefully. "What do you want?"

"Well, anything, really, but especially his old laptop or something."

"Why?"

"He... might have some books stored on it."

"What books?"

I hesitated. Did I really want to tell the man I was looking for a book that was illegal to distribute back on Earth? What else was I going to tell him? *"I was really hoping for some study notes from the lab"* probably wouldn't work.

"I was hoping to find... his Bible." My voice dropped at the end of the sentence.

Mr. Sardis stared. "Why do you need his?"

I felt my palms go clammy. "I... didn't you hear about the virus? Didn't it wipe the systems up here?"

Hope surged. Maybe Mars hadn't been affected. Maybe everything was still here. Maybe...

"Ah... yes," Mr. Sardis stuttered. "But... well... hmm." He propped his elbow on the table and thought a minute. Then he shoved his chair back.

"Wait right here," he said, gesturing with his finger for emphasis.

I did, quite literally, too baffled to go anywhere else. He came back about ten minutes later, waving a reader very similar to my own.

He presented it to me with a grin. "Here you go!"

The metal felt warm in my hands. I squinted at the screen, almost afraid to look—and there it was. A folder labeled "Bible," with each book arranged in order.

I was so elated I almost forgot to ask. But common sense— and disbelief—caught up. "Where did you get this?"

Mr. Sardis popped his jaw. "Erm... Nic made back-ups."

"*Dr. Nic* made back-ups?"

"Yeah. For Cea, I think it was."

For Cea? I couldn't help but remind him, "Doesn't he know transmitting is illegal?"

"Of course. That's why he made copies when the law went into effect. Just in case." Mr. Sardis winked.

I didn't find that comforting. Something wasn't snapping into place. "But... isn't he a Unionist?" That sounded stupid, so I clarified. "Aren't all the colonies up here subject to United policy, too?"

Mr. Sardis laughed. "Well, we would be, if they enforced it." He sauntered back to his chair. "You see, Philli, the United doesn't ask a lot of questions. Not if you've signed the file."

He scooped up his trash. "Don't ask, don't tell. And if they do ask, still don't tell. If you tell the officials what they want to hear, they won't come sticking their noses in your business. Sign the file, submit your annual report, and they think you're being well-behaved Unionists."

I looked down at the screen in my hands. *We figured they can't stop us from thinking about it, and that's what matters, right? It's a relationship, not a religion.*

Mr. Sardis walked towards the cafeteria doors. I followed in a daze. "What do they know!" he boomed. "Up here, I can sing hymns from the rooftop if I want, as long as I shut up when we have official visitors."

If you come to my house, you may keep your Bible. You may pray and worship however you like in your room, and no one will bother you.

Come with me. Come with me.

"Yup, I'm one of you. A Christian! But that's our little secret." He chuckled as he dumped his trash. "So, will that do you?"

"I... yes. Yes, thank you very much." All other thoughts evaporated from my head as I realized what I was holding. I quickly picked a random book and opened it to make sure the words were still there.

See, I have placed before you an open door that no one can shut...

"Ah... one thing," Mr. Sardis added. He rubbed his chin. "Don't connect that to the wifi."

"Doesn't it...?"

"Not automatically. You'd have to go in and add the network."

That's illegal. I looked up at him, but I didn't say it.

He shrugged. "It's old. Been around for a while."

I studied the metal case. It looked newer than my reader. Certainly had more buttons.

"But... shouldn't we send this... to everyone? So they can have the Bible, too?"

"Isn't transmitting illegal?"

I looked down. *That hasn't stopped me before...*

He laid his hand on my shoulder. "Maybe later—once we're sure the virus has been fixed. If we do it now, the virus could corrupt it and we'll just lose it."

That made sense. I looked into his face again. "Thank you."

His brilliant grin returned. "You are welcome, Philli. Anytime you need anything, just ask. There's no need to be shy around us. Up here, we accept you for who you are. That's Dr. Nic's vision. You can worship whom you will. Just keep it down when we've got company, okay?"

He winked, patted my shoulder, and left.

17

I stood for a long time in the hall, just staring at the random page of Revelation I'd opened. My thoughts were a garbled mess of Mr. Sardis's words and streams of Scripture. Eventually, I switched to a different page and began to read.

I probably would have stood there for hours had Cea not stumbled across me.

"What are you doing?"

I almost responded "reading," then caught myself. I held out the reader to show her. "Mr. Sardis copied it for me."

"Where did he... Why did you need one?"

"The virus wiped all the copies on Earth," I reminded her.

She stared blankly. I waited for some explanation, some excuse for why Dr. Nic had copies of illegal books lying around. She shook her head and looked away. "You should have said something."

"How was I supposed to know that..." I sighed and tried to organize my thoughts. "I didn't know if Mars would be... like Earth. If the rules were the same. If Dr. Nic would be like..."

"Nic is *not* like that Ambrose character," Cea snapped. I felt bad for asking.

"Is he a Christian?" I ventured.

"No... sadly." Cea's shoulders drooped.

"Are you?" I looked into her face.

She lifted her gaze to meet mine. "Yes."

"Why didn't you tell me?"

"You didn't ask." She shrugged and abruptly started walking.

I skipped to catch up with her. "You didn't say anything when I mentioned coming from a camp."

"Can you blame me for not wanting to admit that I should be in a camp right now?"

"No," was my ready response. Then, "Why aren't you?"

At this, she smiled and turned to face me. The light in her eyes was comforting. "Nic. That's why he came up here. He's always working to make life better—why else would he specialize in experimental technology? One day he's going to cut us off from the United so everyone can worship in peace, to whomever they worship."

The glint in her eyes turned from comforting to disturbing. "How's he going to do that?" I said carefully.

"By becoming more powerful than they are. That's the only way to cut yourself off from a monster and keep them from assimilating you back in."

Assimilated or removed. "How will he be more powerful?"

Cea opened her mouth, then stopped. Her smile faded as though she realized she had gone too far. "That's... the pet project."

"A secret," I guessed.

"Yeah." She sighed, then shook her head. "But you're not involved. In the meantime, Nic's doing the best he can. As governor, he can make sure we have space to worship, as long as we behave when the United calls."

She laid her hand over the reader screen. "We want you here, Philli. Nic wants everyone to have freedom. You're safe here."

She looked into my face. "Just do what Nic says and you'll be fine."

I looked down at the verses peeking out from behind her hand. *Take their offer while you still can. Take it and run!*

I looked up again. "I want to show this to my father. When will he get off work?"

Cea smiled, gaze returning to normal. "I saw Nic and a few others wandering around the halls just now. I think they're on break."

She turned and pointed. "If you head straight up that way, Gate 34 is on your right. Go through that, then Gate 38. Last I saw them, they were working around meeting room 38D. Just don't go anywhere else and you'll be fine."

"I hope so," I said with a lack of conviction. "But thank you." I started walking in the direction she indicated.

"It will be fine, Phil," she called after me, first loudly, then softly. "It will be fine."

18

I tried to force all other thoughts out of my head as I walked, just concentrating on remembering the directions. 34 on the right, then 38, then 38D. I could remember that.

Remembering on the way over wasn't necessarily the problem. Remembering on the way back could be a different story.

I let out my breath. *Please don't let me get lost again, Lord. I just need to talk to Daddy.* My thoughts perked up as I passed through Gate 34, which was on the right like Cea said it would be. *He'll be so excited to see these, and then I can tell him about...*

My thoughts drooped down again. Daddy didn't know about Ephesus yet. I would have to tell him about seeing Ephesus's room, getting lost, watching all the tapes, talking to Mr. Sardis, and...

This could be a long conversation. Some of this might have to wait until after dinner.

I entered Wing 38. Meeting room 38D was right ahead of me, and the door was shut. No one was in the hall.

I hope they're still down here... and they're not busy! Mustering up my nerves, I walked up to the door and pressed the call button.

There was a moment of silence. *Well, you have to say something!* "Dad... Dr. Smyrna?"

Silence. Static and mumblings. Grumpily, "Who is it?"

Dr. Nic's voice. His terseness made me fumble. "Me... Phil. Philadelphia. Is my father there?"

"Yes." Silence.

"May I speak to him please?"

His response was difficult to hear. "And it can't wait?"

No, actually... "Well, Cea thought he was on break, and I didn't catch him at lunch." *Sorry to involve you, Cea!*

Bitter mutters. He said something—was it directed at me? I couldn't distinguish it. I stood on my toes and leaned my ear closer to the speaker.

I slipped, and my hand brushed the sensor.

I gave a small scream and stumbled back, clutching the reader to keep from dropping it, as the door hissed open. The panel glowed green cheekily.

The men's heated conversation stopped. All the white-coated figures turned and glared at me.

"You are not allowed in here," Dr. Nic informed me thoroughly.

Carnegie frowned. "How did you..."

"It was an accident!" *That's what they all say...* "I bumped the sensor, it..." I shook my finger at the panel.

Dr. Nic strode into the hall and watched as the green circle faded away.

Carnegie crowded behind him. "But she doesn't have access..."

Dr. Nic muttered, "I'm beginning to think that fact is irrelevant."

"Curses," Carnegie spat, and offered a few examples.

The other scientists hovered and murmured, gazing curiously at me. My father calmly emerged from the crowd.

"Phil." He tapped my arm.

"Daddy, I'm sorry… I need to talk to you." I tipped the reader to show him the screen.

His eyes went wide. Lowering his voice, he spoke quickly. "It will have to wait until we're done here." He looked back at the meeting room and frowned.

Somehow I got the impression that he would have gladly abandoned the meeting to talk to me.

"Well, little miss who defies all security systems." Dr. Nic turned away from the panel and crossed his arms.

"Perhaps she should work in security. She might be a genius waiting to happen," Carnegie said without amusement.

The men whispered amongst themselves. Daddy knotted his eyebrows together and glanced at me. *What did you do?* I shrugged honestly.

Dr. Nic tossed his hair and spoke up. "Is there anything else we can do for you?"

I shook my head quickly. "It can wait until you're done. I'm sorry to interrupt—I didn't know you were in a meeting."

My father let go of my arm. I turned.

"In the future, Philadelphia…" Dr. Nic called after me.

I stopped but couldn't bring myself to look back at him.

"You will not bother your father during working hours."

One of the men objected to this. "Heavens, Nic, she interrupted one meeting by accident. What's the crime? You don't mind if my wife visits me during the day."

"Regulations," Dr. Nic snapped. I cringed.

Daddy stared. He said nothing.

"And…" Dr. Nic held me back still. "You will not come around here in the 30s again, do you understand? This is private space for work of which you are not a part."

I ran.

"Tell Cea I will speak with her in half an hour!" he yelled.

I couldn't bring myself to respond. I darted through Gate 38 and fled.

✻

I nearly collided with Cea as I crashed back down the hall towards the dorms.

"Did you find him?" she said, sidestepping to avoid me.

I stopped and panted. "No… yes. They were in a meeting. It will have to wait."

She eyed me. "Sit down." She gestured into a nearby office.

I collapsed in the nearest chair. She shut the door behind us.

"Why were you running?" She walked over and sat behind the desk.

"It felt emotionally appropriate." I drew a long breath and steadied my voice. "Nic said he will speak with you in a half-hour."

Cea frowned, but her eyes were not accusing. "What happened?"

"I accidentally interrupted their meeting."

"How did you manage to do that? Didn't you just use the call button?"

"I did, but… I bumped the sensor, and the door opened." I singed red. "It wasn't supposed to let me in, I gather."

Cea was silent.

"He told me not to go back there, in the 30s…"

"He who?"

"Nic. And he said not to bother my father during work hours anymore."

Cea stared into my eyes. "I'm sorry."

"Regulations," I muttered.

She sighed. "Well, I wouldn't worry about it. You won't have to go back there again."

That was the second time today she'd said that. I stiffened and sat up. "I don't think he really cares about me wandering the halls in the 30s."

She turned to face the computer screen. I kept talking.

"I think he's worried about me accidentally opening doors that were not meant to open for me." I paused. "Like Gate 74."

Cea abruptly started typing on the computer.

"Cea, please..."

She stopped typing, but she didn't look at me. I got up and stood in front of the desk.

"Gate 74 wasn't supposed to let me in, was it?"

She covered her face with her hand, but she answered. "No."

"Does it have to do with Daddy's work?"

"No... not yet anyway. Your father is not allowed in Wing 74 either. Few people are." She looked up at me finally. "Please leave it that way."

I thought a minute. "It's the pet project," I declared.

She swiveled the chair to face the wall, then whispered, "Yes."

She suddenly twirled the chair back around. "Just leave it be, Phil. Please stay away."

"I will."

"Thank you." She sighed.

"Then maybe you can tell me something else."

She looked at me out of the corner of her eye with mixed hopefulness and dread.

"Where are Ephesus's things?"

"Weren't they on the—"

"No. He was just coming back for a visit. A week, two weeks tops. He should have left some stuff behind."

"Didn't... didn't the United send them back to you after his death?"

I could tell by the look in her eyes that she didn't believe her own words. "The United is not that kind."

She stared directly into my face, perhaps unintentionally.

"What did you do with them?" I repeated. I realized how harsh my voice sounded. "Please. It's all I have left of him."

"I... can't tell you."

I wasn't sure whether that meant "I don't know" or "I'm not allowed to say." I was beginning to believe it was the latter.

I searched her gray eyes. They pleaded with me. She wasn't telling me everything, that I knew.

But what she was telling me—it was the truth.

"I'm going to my room."

She nodded. I walked to the door.

She called out to me, voice hushed. "Phil... I'm sorry."

I left.

DR NIC

19

After dinner, I gave my father a detailed synopsis of the day. I wasn't entirely surprised when he said the same thing as Cea.

"Don't go snooping around the halls. Just leave it be."

"I didn't mean to cause trouble."

"I know," he sighed, voice reassuring, "but we must avoid trouble if we can help it. Christians do not need trouble, even in a tolerant place."

"I'm sorry, Dad. I'll stay close to the dorms tomorrow. I'm going to look through more of the security records."

He frowned. "Do you think you can handle more of... him?" His phrasing was awkward.

"I'll manage. I'm going to see if I can find out what they did with his baggage." I looked at him for silent approval.

He pondered before giving it. "Perhaps they destroyed the leftovers."

"If they did, no one will give me a straight answer." My eyes pleaded with him to understand.

He did. He shook his head. "It's a touchy subject. I guess I don't blame them. If I had a tragedy like that on my hands... it wouldn't be my favorite thing to talk about."

That hadn't occurred to me. "Do you think Dr. Nic just doesn't want to remember?"

My father contorted his eyebrows. "I'm... still trying to figure Dr. Nic out. He's... confusing."

I slid closer to him on the couch. "Was work okay?"

"Not entirely," was the somewhat unexpected answer. He sighed wearily.

"What's wrong?"

"Nothing—yet. Nothing I can discuss." He looked down at me. "And you know that when I withhold information from you, it's not to hurt you."

I snuggled close to him. He rubbed my back in silence for a moment.

After a while, I asked again, "May I look at the security tapes and try to find out what happened to his stuff?"

"Yes," he consented, "you may."

*

I didn't catch Cea at breakfast, which was just as well. I wasn't sure I wanted to talk with her. Honestly, I wasn't sure I wanted to tell her what I was doing.

No one was using the security room when I went in. I had several uninterrupted hours to work, during which I did nothing but flip between cameras.

I had a good plan for figuring out what happened to my brother's stuff. I would find the camera that was stationed outside his dorm and watch all the recordings surrounding the day of the accident. Then I would see for sure how much baggage he carried out when he left, and what happened when people went in to clean the room later.

There were only two catches to my plan. The first was that the recordings with the information I needed could have been removed. Cea said some of them had been taken off to investigate the accident.

But I wouldn't know for sure until I watched all the available recordings. To do that I had to figure out which camera corresponded to that hall.

That was the second catch.

I had no idea what numbers I was looking for. Was there even a camera in that hall? It didn't help that I couldn't remember what wing the dorms had been in.

Cea knew, but I wasn't going to ask her right now.

Discouraged or otherwise, I decided to try. After all, I didn't have anything better to do.

After an hour of searching, it occurred to me that I might not even know the hall when I saw it. They all looked the same.

Then I had an idea. I brought up yesterday's records and scrolled through random cameras until I saw myself.

Cea and I were walking out of my room after unpacking. Perfect.

I kept one eye on the display generated in the corner of the room as I pawed through menus. I used guess and check to follow our trail, switching cameras madly in an attempt to keep up.

I managed not to lose track of my ghostly self, and my efforts were rewarded. I sighed aloud with relief when the recording showed Cea opening the door to my brother's dorm and stepping back to give me space. The camera angle was perfect—you could see straight down the hall towards the main door, monitoring everyone that came in and out.

I turned back to the computer and searched for the numbers. Camera 88.3. That didn't sound hard to remember, but I'd better write it down just in case.

I scanned the computer desk, oblivious of my own voice playing over the recording. There was not a single scrap of paper in the room.

I reached down and felt my pouch for my reader. Empty. I must have left it in my room. I sighed.

Leaving the recording running, I ran across the hall to our dorms and fetched it. I opened a blank file and typed with my thumbs as I walked. Not watching where I was going, I collided straight into someone standing in the hallway.

I moaned and mentally told myself I should be smart enough not to walk and write at the same time. I looked up and panicked.

Dr. Nic glared down at me.

"What are you doing?" His voice was unnervingly loud.

"Looking at the recordings," I said hastily, scrambling up.

"For?"

"For?" I repeated dumbly.

"For what?" He was outright shouting now. "What are you looking for?"

"For… for Ephesus."

"Ephesus!"

"My… my brother, sir. He was my brother." My voice hushed, partly because his loudness was scaring me.

"Your brother." He growled and turned away. He didn't seem surprised to hear this information.

I swallowed and waited. He ran a hand through his hair.

"What about your brother?"

Why was that the automatic response? Why, when I spoke of my brother, did everyone demand an explanation? He was my brother—wasn't that enough? Wasn't I entitled to know everything?

I closed my eyes and prayed, hard.

My silence was too long for Dr. Nic. He turned around, glare settling on me again. "What do you want to know?"

"I wanted… I wanted to know what happened to his stuff."

"His stuff?" It was Dr. Nic's turn to repeat me dumbly.

"His things—his baggage. Whatever he left behind when he came back to Earth for a visit. I want his leftover things. They belong to my family and no one will tell me where they are!"

I spoke too quickly—and too harshly. "Do not talk back to me," Dr. Nic spat with venom. "What happened to the baggage after the accident is none of your concern. Your brother's business and his doings here are none of your concern."

It's his assignment, not yours. I took a step backwards.

Dr. Nic turned to the door. "Do not mess with the recordings again." He reached into his pocket and pulled out that disc-gadget.

I sucked in my breath. "But Cea—"

"Cea is not in charge. I am." He snapped the disc on the panel and punched a button.

The panel beeped unhappily. Dr. Nic removed the disc and waved his hand over the sensor. A pause, another beep, and the doors shut, locked for good.

Dr. Nic turned to me again, voice strangely calm. "I expect you will refrain from any further snooping. You have been far too inquisitive for having been here less than 48 hours."

At first I couldn't think of anything to say. My breath rose in my throat, and my volume rose with it. "I was just asking about my brother! He's my brother! And you took him away!"

"I took him away?" His mustache twitched.

"You're the one that requested him, weren't you? You didn't give him a choice! You didn't give my father a choice, either." I took two more steps backwards.

"No," he said without regret. "I'm also the one that called for you."

I froze.

"The commander didn't want to let you come. Said it was against 'regulations.' But I didn't think it was right to leave a young girl in the hands of strangers. Your brother was an adult," he cut off my excuses before I could think them, "you're a minor. And you have nobody. I didn't think that was right."

I backed away. He advanced and narrowed the gap. "If you don't want to be here, you don't have to stay. I could... send you back to Earth." The threat was calm, flat like a sheet of razor-sharp ice.

I sucked in several gasps. "I'm… sorry. I'm sorry."

He was smiling again, but it wasn't an encouraging smile. I didn't feel like he was forgiving me for my disrespectfulness—I felt like he was accepting my surrender.

"It's all right," he said, and he sounded reasonably truthful about it. "Just stay out of my way." His smile deepened, eyes glittering. "Just keep your head down, Philadelphia, and no one will know the difference."

I turned and ran for the dorms.

20

I went to lunch, but only because I didn't want anyone to worry. After pretending to eat, I went back to the dorms and huddled on the couch, praying. Or trying to.

A knock on the door interrupted my stewing.

I forced myself to get up and hit the call button. "Who is it?" I said, making a mental list of people I was willing to talk to right now.

"Cea." The line fuzzed with her breath.

She wasn't on the list, but I answered anyway. "Come in."

She did—and shut the door again.

She regarded the keypad. "Lock it, please."

I stood up. "Why?"

"So no one else comes in."

I didn't move towards the panel. "Why?"

"Ephesus."

I walked over and tapped the keys to lock the door.

I turned towards her. She was staring at me, eyes narrowed.

"How intelligent are you?" Her voice was bitter.

"What?"

"I suppose how patient and trusting are you might be a more accurate question."

"Define trust."

"If I... tell you something... about your brother. About Ephesus. Are you... will you wait... with the questions? Can you trust me until I can explain more? Will you do as I say and not try to figure it out yourself?"

I stared at her. Her eyes softened; her voice faded.

"Can you take it one step at a time?"

*

"There are two rules."

I ran to keep up with her. Cea was walking briskly, but aimlessly—or so it seemed. She'd weave down a hall, then turn, then turn again. North for a few halls, then south again. If she was trying to get me lost, she'd succeeded five minutes ago.

"First rule is... you must never speak of anything you hear or see today—anything—with anyone."

How cliché! My heart sank. I couldn't go along with this, not if I couldn't...

"Except your father."

I looked up at her. She kept walking, but she gazed into my eyes.

"You may speak of it with your father—but only your father! And only in your private quarters. Mention it anywhere else, and it could end up on a public security tape."

She turned away from me and picked up the pace.

"The other rule... you must never go where I am about to take you. Not by yourself. Never come near it. If someone mentions it, act like it doesn't exist. Never, ever come back without me. And don't ask me to come! I will bring you when it's safe, and that will be few and far between."

Her voice cracked. "This is going to be hard, Phil. I'm warning you, this is not going to be easy on you—or your father."

I stared up the hall ahead of us. "Where are we going?"
It was a moment before she replied.
"Wing 74."

21

Wing 74. "The pet project."

"Yes."

"Which I'm not supposed to know about."

"Yes."

"What does that have to do with—"

"Some questions must wait for later!"

She halted at a junction and glanced up the halls. Silence.

She outright ran. I followed as fast as I could. Our boots seemed loud—so loud. Why did that make me nervous?

The halls began to look vaguely familiar—or did they? Then we entered that unsettling wing, that open space with nothing but Gate 72 and 73.

And 74.

Cea strode across the hall towards Gate 74. She held up her hand—then stopped. She looked back at me.

"Go ahead."

I nervously obeyed. Cea waited. Did the system pause on purpose? Then it flashed green.

Cea shoved me in and whisked me down the hall.

"Most of these doors are locked, but one day they'll hook to a maze of new halls. Only one door works right now. A."

"It's not marked," I said as she stopped in front of a gate. I glanced back up the hall and counted the doors—6th down.

"Not from this side."

She opened the door. I already knew that it wouldn't work for me—I tried all the doors the first time I came down Wing 74.

That did not explain why Gate 74 opened for me in the first place.

I subconsciously expected the depths of Wing 74 to be something fantastical. It ought to be—I had every right to expect something extraordinary.

But somehow I wasn't surprised to find that the hall on the other side of the door was... normal.

It looked like the rest of the base.

I glanced at the door as it closed behind us. It was indeed marked *A*.

I didn't get a tour. Cea shoved me into the first door on the right. It was a meeting room, an unfinished one. The walls and ceiling were sealed in and half of a bench was bolted to the back wall. The keypad was dark; Cea dragged the door almost shut with her hands.

"Wait here." And she was off running again.

I stumbled over to the bench and sat down, gripping it with my fingers. The only light came in a sharp shaft through the crack in the door. I scooted down the bench until I was completely in darkness. For some reason, I didn't want to sit in the only shade of light.

Cea soon returned with a second set of footsteps. Her voice was sharp. "You have twenty minutes—use it wisely. I have to get her back and edit the security tapes before Nic returns."

She shoved the door open and manually flicked on the light.

And there he stood.

Dark fluffy hair, absorbent eyes, flat face that only loosely concealed a smile. Unbuttoned lab coat, brown pants, clomping shoes with a scuff on the toe. Not a piece of him was missing.

I knew instantly that I was looking at Ephesus. I never doubted that.

But I utterly doubted that he was real.

Cea threw a quick glance at us and was gone, leaving the door cracked only a millimeter.

"Use it wisely," she said again. Her footsteps retreated.

I stared at him. His eyes were large, but his face was calm—as though his eyes were just widened to take me in faster. He didn't seem that surprised to see me here.

He couldn't be real.

"Philli," he said, "Philadelphia."

A perfect recording.

I stood up. "Why."

"Why what?"

"Why all this trouble… for a hologram?"

"A hologram?"

I stepped towards him. "A hologram. A recording. Robot?" I tipped my head back and looked into his face. "You're not real."

His eyes blurred, though his face did not move. He extended his hand. "Try it."

I remembered touching his hologram in the security tape—and having my fist go right through. This version looked thicker.

I gazed at his hand. Slowly, I brought mine down.

Our palms contacted.

I drew my hand back and did it again. He caught and pinched my hand this time.

I looked into his eyes again. "You're dead," I whispered, but my tiny voice testified to the truth.

"I'm alive."

"You're alive," I repeated. One gasping breath, one shake—one moment of elated terror. Then I screamed.

"Ephesus!"

"Philli!" His voice was a teary wail, and it was the most beautiful sound in the world.

He hugged me. He swept me up in his arms and held me, kissed me, sat down in the middle of the floor and cradled me, muttering in my ear.

He wasn't dead.

That one fact ignited a hundred questions, some I had already been asking myself. But the one answer was worth them all.

Ephesus was alive.

Like Cea said, some questions could wait.

22

But Ephesus didn't make me wait long.

"It's okay…" he sat me down on the floor across from him, "if you ask questions now."

"What… what can you tell me?" I started.

"What did Cea tell you?"

"Nothing. She just asked… if she told me something about my brother… could I save the questions for later? One step at a time. She made me promise…"

"What?"

"…never to tell anyone…"

"Never. No one."

"…except Daddy…"

He leaned forward, dark eyes brewing. "Tell him everything."

"…and only in our private quarters."

"Never breathe a word of it in the halls—anywhere. The tapes. They hear everything."

"And… never come back here again." I blinked. "I see what she meant now. About it being hard."

He gripped my shoulders. "No—never! Not without her. She's the only one that can make sure it's safe. Not even for me, Phil, never come close. Never tread near Wing 74. Pretend like it doesn't exist. If anyone mentions it, act like you know nothing."

He shook me. "I'll be here. Don't worry about me. I'm safe."

"Are you?" I gazed into his eyes.

He returned the challenge. "I am—honestly. All this time I've never been hurt and never lacked anything. Nic... he's not that bad, most days. Really, Philli, I'm safe. I'm comfortable and I'm thinking of you. Now I can pray... and know you're praying for me, too."

"Have you been...?"

"Every day. Or almost."

"Did you know I was here?"

"Yes." He looked away. "When you wandered into Wing 74 yesterday... I saw the security tape. You were... so close. So... far."

I touched his knee. "You're locked in here, aren't you?"

His head bobbed in a barely perceptible nod.

"Why?"

"Mainly, so no one knows I'm here."

"So everyone believes you're dead?"

"Exactly."

"The transfer...?"

"Staged. No one was on it."

"The other passengers?"

"All down here, plus a few others."

"Doing...?"

"Working. For Nic."

"The pet project."

"That's what Cea calls it."

"It must be a secret."

"The defining factor."

"Illegal?"

"Effectively. The United didn't like it, told him to stop. That's why he had to move it underground... and 'kill' scientists to stock the lab." He sighed.

"What is it?" I dared to ask.

"I... don't want to give you the details."

I searched his face. "Don't want to?"

"I don't want to even think the details, let alone scar you with them."

"What?" I repeated, a little taken aback by his harsh tone.

"I don't want to try and explain it right now." He turned away.

I thought of a gentle conversation changer. "I don't understand most of the lab gibberish anyway."

He smiled, that surge of warmth I had missed for so many years. His voice softened. "I love you, Philadelphia."

I hugged him again. "I love you, too."

Footsteps approached down the hall. Ephesus held me at arm's length and spoke quickly.

"Tell Dad everything—everything! Make sure he knows. Make sure he knows! I'm alive—I'm okay. And I love him. Tell him I love him!"

I nodded. Cea grunted, and the door grated open. We stood up; Ephesus kissed my forehead. I squeezed him around the waist.

"I'm sorry, but we've got to clear. Ephesus, get back to work. Remember—speak of this to no one. Make no notes anywhere, not even on your personal computer. There must be no record of this event anywhere on the base. I've got the security tapes."

Ephesus nodded and breezed out of the room. He paused in the hall and glanced back.

"Cea... thank you."

She looked at him, then glanced down. "You're welcome." She grabbed my hand. "Phil, quickly."

I threw one glance back as she hauled me through Gate A.

Ephesus caught it—and smiled.

I smiled back.

✳

I didn't speak until we had fled into the 60s, which seemed far enough away to me.

"Thank... you..." I gasped, for she insisted on running.

"No more!" was her harsh reply.

I silenced until we reached Wing 45. Then I ventured an indirect question.

"When will my father return?"

I wondered if she caught the implications. "He and Nic should be getting back in about an—"

"We docked half an hour ago."

I yelled. However, I had every right, as I suddenly ran into him.

Dr. Nic watched me tumble to the floor. "That is the second time you've run into me today, Philadelphia."

"I'm sorry, sir. I... don't watch where I'm going." I hoped I looked startled—not frightened.

He did frighten me. More every time I saw him. More every time I learned something new about him.

Cea tried not to pant. "Sorry, Nic, I started it."

He looked at her. "And since when does my controlled sister run anywhere?"

She crossed her arms. "We were having fun."

"Doing what? I thought I told you no more snooping." The latter sentence was directed at me with a scowl.

Cea came to my defense. "We weren't snooping. It's exploring."

I cringed at how juvenile that sounded. Cea, to her credit, continued seamlessly. "She's with me. And I know where to go."

I knew that actually meant *"I know where not to go."*

He looked down at me.

What do you want me to say? "'Exploring' is what she calls it. I have no idea where we are."

He was not amused. "Wing 45. Four gates straight that way is the main hall. Your quarters are on the other side."

I took that as a hint.

I stood up. "Thank you, Cea. I'm going to find my father."

She nodded and forced a smile. I copied, hoping it was natural. "I'll see you after dinner," she said.

I wondered if that was a promise. I waved and ran off.

Dr. Nic spoke before I was out of earshot.

"Do you want them to stay together?"

"Yeah?"

"Then act accordingly."

He stomped off. Cea stayed. She looked up and saw me, hesitating there. At first her gaze was white, wide—then it narrowed into a bitter glare.

I fled.

*

Needless to say, I shocked my father on a number of levels with my report after dinner. It was a wonder he could understand it at all—I kept mixing up the events, and my voice wobbled between a tearful sob and an excited shriek.

I finally reached the end and drew a long breath. "And he wanted me to tell you that he loves you. Both of us."

My father echoed the sigh. His shoulders quivered. For a second, he turned away from me and didn't say anything. I hugged him.

"God... brought him back. All that time... God was saving him." I heard the tears in his voice.

I sat back and found his hand. "Cea said she'll take you to visit him as soon as she can."

Daddy pushed crumpled hair off his forehead with his other hand. "I think Dr. Nic will be arranging a meeting soon enough."

"Dr. Nic? But he doesn't want..."

Daddy looked into my face and declared bluntly, "He wants me to join the project."

I realized I wasn't breathing and took a quick gasp. "The pet project?"

My father nodded. "It's the sole reason he called me up here. He thinks my lab expertise is the missing piece to completing a certain phase. Something about Red Rain."

"He… already told you about it? But it's a secret. No one's supposed to know."

"No one's supposed to *tell*."

"But if he doesn't have you locked up, couldn't you tell?"

"I guess he figures I won't. Not when he could send my daughter back to Earth on the next flight."

I waited, eyes wide.

"I, unlike the average Unionist, have nothing to gain from alerting the authorities. If I ruin Nic's project, I go back to Earth to be persecuted. If I stay, I live in tolerance. All my family is up here."

"Which was not the case with Ephesus a few years ago." I connected the dots.

My father squeezed my hand. I rested my head against his shoulder for a moment before looking back into his face.

"Do you want to join?"

"I want to stay," he said emphatically. "I don't know if I want to join. I need to hear more about the project. I'm not sure what I'm dealing with."

"Ephesus doesn't like it," I offered, remembering my brother's cryptic harshness.

"Would you be pleasantly disposed to a project if you'd been kidnapped and forced to work on it?"

"Um… no."

"Nic hasn't given me many details yet. I know it's chemical-related, but what the chemicals are for I haven't figured out. We'll have to talk more. I have a few days, at least."

He tipped my chin up. "This information is confidential. Some of the other scientists don't know about the project, I gather. Tell no one."

"Except Ephesus."

I watched the tears pool in the corners of his eyes. "Tell him everything," he whispered.

I hugged him and allowed myself to release the tears I'd been bottling all afternoon.

Ephesus

23

After the adventure of my first two days at the base, I was amazed that the next two days were completely uneventful. I actually succeeded in "keeping my head down." No one gave me suspicious glances—not even Nic—and I didn't stumble through any more locked doors.

I didn't receive any new information, either. Daddy didn't speak any more of his work, and Cea didn't mention Ephesus or Wing 74 at all. Even though I thought of my brother constantly, I managed not to ask—and I found that he was right. It was comforting to remember that he was only a few halls away.

I filled my days by catching up on my Bible study and writing a long email to Cami—Cea promised to help me get it through the commander. Even though I had to resist the urge to tell her about Ephesus, I found letter-writing to be very distracting. I was caught completely off-guard when Cea came in and announced I could spend a half-hour with Ephesus.

I didn't object.

"I'm sorry I can't get your dad down here. It's a lot harder, because after-hours is usually when Nic is in Wing 74. But that might soon be a non-issue." Her voice perked up, causing me to look at her. She was smiling happily.

Suspicion prevented me from smiling. She must have taken that as a prompt to explain. "I hear—don't quote me on this—that Nic wants your dad to work with Ephesus. That means you'll all get to live here, and we won't have to hide anymore. You can stay."

I didn't think I should tell her what my dad and I had discussed. "We want to," I whispered.

She paused to let me open Gate 74 again. It still worked.

"Who has access to this door?" I asked as we went through.

Cea wrinkled her brow. "Nic, Carnegie, myself... I think all the scientists that are down here have access too, because they helped build it before it was locked off."

She opened Gate A. "Only Nic, Carnegie, and I have access to this one, though. A couple of other scientists know, but they don't have access. Nic has to take them down."

Cea led me to the left this time, to a door across the hall labeled LAB 1. She waved her hand over the sensor, and it refused her. She pressed the call button. "Ephesus, it's me."

"Sorry," came the response, and the door opened. My brother stood there, balancing three test tubes in his hands. He spotted me and beamed. "Philli!" Then he frowned and glanced at Cea. "Cea, she can't be in a lab. Nic reviews all the records—"

"It's fine," Cea assured him, shoving me in. "Nic took the camera for this lab down for repairs this morning. You're clear. But you only have about 30 minutes."

She turned to go, then glanced back and smiled. "Have fun. Don't blow anything up."

I stared after her until she disappeared down a hall, wondering if I should let that admonition concern me.

"Close the door and hit lock, just in case. If someone stumbles by... at least that buys us a minute." My brother staggered over to a table and deposited his tubes.

"Who will be able to get in when it's locked?"

"Just me and Dr. Nic. Who, I suppose, is the person we are most worried about... Lock it anyway."

I did as I was told. I turned around and watched my brother carefully arrange his tubes in a holder. The table was cluttered nearly to the overflowing with a multicolored chaos of glass and chemicals.

He wiped his hands on his coat and came to hug me. "It's good to see you again, and so soon. Cea's in a good mood today."

"What did she mean about 'not blowing anything up'?"

Ephesus turned and gestured at the table. "Because in this room we have the components for a bomb."

There was something about that information that irked me to the core.

"Bomb?" I finally squeaked.

Ephesus sighed and ran a hand through his hair. "Yeah. Big ones. Not all of the pieces are here, but you could create a... disturbance, which we don't need."

I decided to stay a safe distance away from the table. I followed him carefully and watched from a few feet away as he went back to work.

"Does Dr. Nic's plan include bombs?"

Ephesus nodded. "Several. And that's only part of it. Nic wants to have multiple options available."

"Options?"

"So if bombing Earth full of holes doesn't work, he can try something else to get them to back off."

"Them?"

"The United." He paused and glanced back at me. "Has Cea told you anything?"

"Only that Nic wants to break from..." I halted. Everything snapped together. Painfully. *One day he's going to cut us off from the United... By becoming more powerful than they are. That's the only way to cut yourself off from a monster and keep them from assimilating you back in.*

Ephesus looked into my eyes and nodded to confirm my fears.

I swallowed. "And then what?"

"Utopia. In theory. He wants political freedom, which includes religious freedom. Or so he claims." He turned back to the table. "I'll believe it when I see it. And I hope I don't have to see it."

"Why?" For some reason, I felt bad that the first thought that ran through my head was: *Don't we want to break from the United? Don't we want religious freedom?*

"Because I don't want to see what happens when Nic uses this stuff." Ephesus poured two tubes together and watched the liquid change color. "The bombs are a rather small and inconsequential part of his plan, in the grand scheme of things."

He looked up at the ceiling. "That's why I'm working on bombs and not something... worse."

I decided now was a good time to update him on the developments. "Nic wants Dad to join the project."

Ephesus nearly dropped the glass bottle he was holding. "What?" He whipped around.

"He told Daddy about it. Not all of the details, but a lot of the technical stuff."

"Why?" Ephesus looked as confused as I had felt when Daddy told me.

"Things are different with Daddy. He doesn't have anything to gain by alerting the United. All his family is up here."

Ephesus took a step back and braced himself against the edge of the table. He cradled his forehead with his other hand.

"If he says no, he gets sent back to Earth," I offered. "Or... I get sent back to Earth."

"I know." Ephesus looked up again. "Why does he want Dad?"

"He thinks Daddy has the last piece to the project. Something about Red Rain?"

"No," Ephesus breathed, so quietly I wasn't sure if I heard him right.

"No what?"

"No!" He lunged, making the table rock. He grabbed my shoulders. I nearly fell over with the force, but he didn't seem to notice.

"No! No! Tell him *no!*"

"Him who?" I tried to keep calm.

"Dad! Tell him no! Tell him not to accept. He can't accept."

"But, Ephesus, why—"

"Philli," his voice cut in and forced me to focus on him. "Do you know what acid rain is?"

"Well, yes, but—"

"Can you imagine that... with an intensity that can melt metal?"

"What?"

Ephesus let go of me. He turned around to gaze at the table of chemicals. "Red Rain. It's the last phase of Nic's project. It's a concentration of chemicals that can turn normal precipitation— even, in some places, just high humidity—into an acid strong enough to melt metal, let alone scald and kill living beings. It's those chemicals... and the methods to distribute them as gases. To *subtly* distribute them."

I didn't say anything. I didn't know what to say.

Ephesus's voice hardened. "Tell Dad he doesn't want to join the project. Tell Dad he doesn't want to join the project, unless he wants to be responsible for raining fire and brimstone on half of Earth. Tell him he doesn't want to join unless he wants my *guilt*."

He choked off and covered his face with his hands.

I stepped closer to him. "Did you... work on..."

"Yes. When I first came here, I did a bit of work, not knowing what it was. When I learned more, I tried to stop it. I was the one that got the United curious. I was the one that made Nic take it underground."

I felt a strange sense of warmth at that statement. "I'm proud of you," I said honestly.

He gave a sort of chuckled snort. "Yeah. Nic said he'd send me back to Earth—I told him I wanted to go. I had family down there. So he sent me. Only... my transit 'exploded.'"

"He wouldn't let you go. Did you know too much?"

"Yes, but I still haven't decided whether it's because I knew too much about the project or because he needed my brains, as arrogant as that sounds. Thankfully, I didn't have the knowledge necessary to advance Red Rain, so I got moved to another phase. I agreed to work on another phase, as long as it wasn't Red Rain." He let out his breath. "I wish I hadn't agreed."

"What would he have done?"

Ephesus shrugged. "I don't know. Killing me—for real—wouldn't have gained him anything. But what else was I supposed to do? There's no point in turning back now. This phase is almost done."

"Have you been working on this for two years?" I gazed at the table.

"No. I did some bombs, some guns..." He gestured casually. "My first project was a virus."

"What?" The word came out in a strangled gasp.

"Computer virus," he replied. "Nic wanted something that could wipe out Earth's data, to cripple them digitally if we had to. Another scientist and I did it."

I looked for something—anything—to grip. My hand found the pouch around my waist. I felt both readers thump against me.

"We switched it up, though. We set it so that the virus would only delete data that contained the letters 'Nic,' with a capital."

Ephesus actually grinned. "Nic's not good at coding, so he can't tell. We figured we'd delete a few books and web pages about Nicolas's, but at least Earth wouldn't lose enough data to send them back to the Dark Age."

He looked back at me. "I wouldn't do that to Earth. I wouldn't do that to you."

I was surprised to find that my breath was still coming in regular gasps. I touched my forehead, trying to process.

Ephesus squinted at me. "What's wrong, Phil? Are you all right?"

"You… wrote the virus," was the only thing I could think of to say. Perhaps it was the only thing that needed to be said.

He shrugged.

"Why?" I looked into his eyes, searching for logic, an explanation—an apology.

I didn't find any. "Nic won't have to use it," Ephesus said. "Once Earth hears of Red Rain, they'll cower in terror. Nic might have to demonstrate a little, but… He wouldn't bomb the unassimilated camps. Not intentionally, because of Cea. The virus won't be necessary. None of this will be necessary if he doesn't complete Red Rain. He won't try anything early."

I felt hot and flushed. I rubbed my cheeks. "Yes, he will."

He shook his head. "Don't worry, he won't. Trust me. I know Nic."

"He already did." I took a step back.

His face softened. "What's wrong, Phil?" He stepped towards me, but I kept the distance between us. I almost sighed aloud when Cea's voice echoed through the speaker.

"I'm sorry, Phil, but we've got to go. Nic changed his schedule."

I ran for the door and waved my hand over the sensor. I knew it would open.

As the doors parted, I stole a glance back at Ephesus. He stared, dumbfounded.

I didn't wait for Cea to say anything and raced across the hall to Gate A. If she noticed my impatience, she didn't question it. She walked up beside me and opened the gate.

"Phil, wait!" Ephesus darted to the doorway of Lab 1.

I stopped but didn't turn around.

He drew in a breath—then let it out. He finally spoke, a little quietly. "Tell Dad. Tell him not… to."

"He won't," I said confidently. Then I strode through the doors and left him behind.

It wasn't until we were a few wings away that I realized I might have forfeited my last chance to say goodbye.

I managed to hold it back until we reached Wing 1. Cea asked questions, but I didn't answer. She finally left me alone in the dorms.

And then I cried.

24

I was eating lunch with Cea when he came for me. He sent Carnegie.

"The doctor will see you."

I stood up, even though I didn't want to. He glared down at me, eyes glinting like polished steel.

Cea burst into tears.

Carnegie grabbed my arm and dragged me out of the room. "I'm sorry! I'm sorry!" Cea wailed at no one in particular.

"Assimilated or removed!" Carnegie shot back.

He hauled me across the base. I expected him to take me to Dr. Nic's office, but he didn't. He wound down to the very tip of the base, to the docking bay.

A little treaded car was parked in the wing. The doors were open.

Dr. Nic stood in the middle of the room, arms crossed. A suitcase—mine—sat at his feet.

"No," I said.

"Yes," was his reply. "Get in."

I wasn't sure if I walked, or if Carnegie shoved me. I neared the open doors and suddenly stopped, bracing my hands against the side of the car.

The inside of the vehicle was empty.

"Daddy," I breathed.

I heard groaning. I glanced over my shoulder. Gate 74 stood there, open.

Daddy lay inside, crumpled against one of those unmarked doors. He held his head and mumbled.

Ephesus stood over him, gripping his shoulders.

"No, Daddy!" I ran for him.

Gate 74 began to shut.

I heard a familiar voice—not Dr. Nic's, or Carnegie's—behind my head. "It's his assignment, not yours! Regulations!"

Ephesus saw me. "Philli!" he screamed.

Daddy had no voice. He looked up—our eyes met through the shrinking crack between the doors.

I screamed.

I slammed into the door just as it sealed shut. I quickly turned and flapped my hand over the sensor.

Access denied.

I whipped around. "No, please!"

Dr. Nic wasn't there anymore. Carnegie was walking away, cackling, "System fixed!"

Someone else stood next to my suitcase.

Commander Ambrose.

"Regulations!" he snarled. "Regulations!" He waved his pistol at me.

Assimilated or removed. Assimilated or removed.

"Come on, honey, we missed you."

I pinched my eyes shut. "No, you didn't!"

But it wasn't the commander speaking. It was a buttery voice, a happy voice. A compromising voice.

Mrs. Nolan emerged from the car.

"Come on, darling, we've been waiting for you." She beckoned to me. "We still want you. Join our family. Join our family."

"I don't want to!" I clenched my fists and backed away. I ran into someone else—a large someone.

He scooped me up in his arms.

"No!" I shrieked. I fought—but could only hit air.

"Shh," Mrs. Nolan stroked my hair, "it's just my husband."

I looked into his face. He gazed back. Soft blondish hair, eyes so calm, so relaxed, so... relaxed...

"You've made the right choice, daughter."

"You're not my dad," I hissed. I wanted to yell—but my voice came out in a whisper. I could hardly hear it. Could anyone else hear it?

Commander Ambrose answered me. "He is now. Take it or leave it."

Take it while you still can! Take their offer and run!

I couldn't resist. I felt as if I were floating.

He set me down in a seat inside the car. He moved where I couldn't see him. I felt alone. No, there was someone next to me.

Cea.

She sat, twisting white hands. Tear streaks ran down her cheeks. A duffel lay between her feet.

"Cea!" I cried.

She noticed me. Her eyes widened. "Phil! Philadelphia!"

She stood up. I reached for her—she was right there, but our hands didn't touch. Her voice rose in panic.

"Phil! Philadelphia! Phil! *Philli!*"

Suddenly, I hit the floor.

Everything was dark—and so hot! I groped—and felt a rug beneath my fingers.

I froze, forcing my gasping breaths to steady. Cea was still calling my name, but more calmly. Her voice warbled over a speaker.

The speaker at the door of our apartment.

I scrambled up—and tripped. A blanket tangled my feet—the throw blanket from the couch. I struggled away and stood, panting, in the middle of the room. Sweat ran down my neck.

"Phil? Philadelphia? Are you in there? Phil!"

I stumbled over to the door. I flicked on the lights and jammed the thermostat as cold as it would go.

I blindly waved my hand to open the door and sank to my knees.

Cea came in, took one look, and quickly shut the door behind her. "Phil!" She knelt beside me.

I quivered on the floor, listening to the fans churn wildly, letting the cold air swoop down my arms. It felt chilled, frozen—and I relished it.

Cea waited a moment. "What's wrong?"

"Why are you here?"

"I wondered why you weren't at breakfast." She paused. "It's after 10."

I moaned.

"Phil, what's wrong?"

"Nothing, everything… yes… no. Part of it. You're not on a transfer to go back to Earth."

"Me? Why would I…"

"I don't know. That part didn't make sense. Most of the rest did. Too much sense. Too… plausible." I shivered.

"Why were you sleeping on the couch?"

That was an excellent question. I concentrated, and the memories returned. "I was up with Dad before he went to work. I guess I dozed off."

Cea pinched a damp tangle of my hair between her fingers. "Are you sure you're not ill?"

"Reasonably."

She let go of my hair. Slowly, she stood up.

"Wash up and come down to get something to eat."

*

For once, the cafeteria was actually deserted. Not a single soul was there. The buffet had already been taken down, but Cea ordered a little something for me.

Despite myself, I figured I had ignored enough of my meals lately in favor of emotional trauma. It wasn't healthy. I ate everything Cea gave me even though I didn't have any pleasure in it.

Cea waited until I was nearly done before speaking. "I'm sorry. These past few days…" She sighed. "It's mostly my fault."

"No," I said emphatically. "I'm glad you were honest with me. You're the only one outside my family who has been in a very long time."

I took a sip of water before continuing. "Thank you. Without you, I would have never seen Ephesus again."

She stared at me. "You're… welcome," she said finally.

Abruptly, her eyes lit up. "But I have good news." She glanced around and lowered her voice. "Nic is settling the job details with your father today. If all goes well, your father will be able to see your brother, and then you can visit whenever you want. There won't be any more secrets. You'll just have to act surprised when Nic takes you to see Ephesus for the first time." She winked.

I swallowed, then finished my piece of toast before replying. I needed the time to formulate my thoughts.

Cea frowned at my silence. I wiped my lips and looked up at her. "My father isn't taking the job."

"What?" she said, more of a gasp than a word.

"My father will not accept the position. He will not work on 'Red Rain.' It goes against his ethics—our ethics."

"But…" Her face crashed. She closed her eyes, drew a breath, and looked at me again. She spoke quickly but calmly.

"I know. I know how it looks. I hate it, it's the worst part of Nic's operation. That's why I'm not down there, helping."

Apparently Nic wouldn't force his own sister to work, but he'd kidnap a dozen scientists and forge their deaths.

"But I promise you—he won't have to use it. He just has to prove to the United that he could beat them in a war, so they'll stay away. Then he can expand the base, open the doors to colonists, and establish a new world—on Mars!—with religious freedom. It will be like America in the old millennium. It will be perfect."

"Perfect?" I ate my last forkful of eggs.

"I won't have to worry anymore—you won't have to worry anymore. We won't have to play 'perfect obedient Unionists.'"

"I never have been a very model Unionist," I mused, more to myself than to her.

"Philli…" She reached out to me. "Please. Just give him a chance. It's the only way we'll break from the United and find freedom. If we don't do something, it will just get worse."

Evildoers and impostors will go from bad to worse, deceiving and being deceived… "Dr. Nic's already made it worse."

"What? How?" She frowned.

"The virus. He made that. My brother made that."

"Oh." She paused, and I thought I'd made my point. Then she stiffened and rattled off again. "That was an accident. He was testing it on a private cloud, and something went wrong. It didn't do what it was supposed to, and it got onto a wifi-connected device. He has to fix it."

Fix it? So he can release it again and do worse damage?

"But he said he'll repair the damage. He's got back-ups of a lot of the lost lost data on Wing 74's cloud."

"When?"

"After his plan is done. After everyone knows about Red Rain and he doesn't have to explain why he's got a system totally disconnected from the United's surveillance."

I arranged my trash on my empty plate in a weird pattern. "After he's desecrated half of Earth with chemical warfare."

"He won't have to use Red Rain."

"He didn't have to use the virus." I stood up.

She didn't follow at first. "It's the only way. The United is too big for any other method to work. Can you think of another way?"

I pondered that as I stacked my empty dishes. "No."

Cea's shoulders relaxed slightly.

"But that doesn't mean I'm going to choose the wrong way."

She didn't say anything. She didn't move at all, not even blink.

I looked her in the eyes again. "Daddy and I prayed about it. He's going to refuse the commission. He will not work on Red Rain."

"That's the only reason Nic called him up here," Cea declared.

"I know."

Her voice grew bitter. "He will probably send you back to Earth."

"I know."

"You'll never see Ephesus again."

I turned away. *Not if I can pull this off.*

She must have thought my lack of response was consent. "Nic won't let him go. He's still dead."

He knows too much. So do I.

She pushed harder. "If you try something, he might kill Ephesus for real."

Not if we're careful. Not if God helps us. God, please! I closed my eyes and rehearsed my daddy's warning. *"Yes, you may, but don't try it until I know how Dr. Nic will react. He does have weapons."*

Cea stood up and walked towards me. "Please give Nic a chance. Please reconsider."

"We won't." I turned around to face Cea again. "Please, let me see Ephesus. Now. As soon as possible."

She stared. I couldn't read her expression. "One last time," I pleaded.

She squinted. I wondered if she could tell that *I* was now the one keeping secrets.

Whether she knew or not, she relented. "Okay. I'll make it happen. Wait in your dorms until it's safe."

She started walking away.

"Cea," I called after her. She paused. "Thank you."

She glanced over her shoulder, gaze soft. "You're welcome." Then she left.

I pinched my eyes shut and prayed. *Please, God... we have one chance.* One chance.

I reached into my pouch. Both readers were there, ready.

25

Ephesus was working in Lab 1 again. I didn't wait for him to set down what he was holding before I hugged him from behind.

"Philli!" He stumbled forward and dropped something on the floor.

"I don't know how long you have," Cea said from the doorway. "Nic will be busy as long as he's talking with your father. But if your father refuses the job... the meeting could be short."

I lifted my head and looked at her. "Thank you again."

She didn't say anything. She just nodded and fled.

I ran over to the door and locked it behind her. I turned around to find Ephesus squinting at me.

"The door. Yesterday. You didn't have access," he declared bluntly.

I beamed. "No, but you do. And I'm your sister. By blood." I held up my palm.

He stepped forward and pressed his larger fingers against mine. Slowly, he smiled.

I walked over to the table and pulled the two readers out of my pocket.

Ephesus sighed. "Phil…" he said, voice heavy. "I'm sorry. I… asked Nic about the virus."

I set my personal reader on the table and turned the one from Mr. Sardis on.

"He wants me to fix it. I won't do it, this time."

"You won't have to. Not if you give me evidence." I thrust the device at him.

He skeptically took it. "What?"

"Give me some files. Something techy and revealing. If Dr. Nic sends us back to Earth, I'll have evidence to show the United and prove there's something up here they should investigate." I looked into his face.

He stared, then beamed. He looked down at the device and started toggling menus. "Is he saying no?"

"He's saying no. If Dad doesn't get to see you…"

"You can tell him that I love him," he smiled and typed on the reader's pad, "and I'll be here when the United calls."

The device beeped. He looked down at it and frowned. "Where did you get this?"

"Mr. Sardis gave it to me. Because… I didn't have a Bible." I clasped my hands behind my back.

"It's connected to Wing 74's private wifi. It can access all of the base-level data."

I wasn't sure if I should feel stupid for not realizing that earlier, or perturbed that I had been carrying the secrets for chemical warfare around in my pocket. "Well… that's terrifying."

"I'm not surprised you didn't notice. I doubt the range on the wifi is very far."

I thought for a moment. "What if we just connected it to the public wifi and copied over some files?"

Ephesus shook his head. "All of Wing 74's devices are specially coded to make connecting to a new network very difficult. The access codes are Nic's heavily-guarded secret, for obvious reasons."

My spirits fell again, only to surge back up with a rush of adrenaline. The cycle was getting vicious. "We can use this." I snatched my personal reader off the table. "This is just a regular device. Can we download something I can copy over?"

Ephesus didn't respond. He was frowning.

"Ephesus?"

He shushed me harshly. Cautiously, he set the reader on the table and eased over to the door. He listened for a second, then reached up and hit the call button.

Dr. Nic's voice blared over the speaker, muddled with Carnegie's.

And then I heard Dad.

I choked. Ephesus stuck his arm out, and I instinctively stopped breathing. I forced myself to hold still, panicked prayers spiraling through my head.

"I question the wisdom of kidnapping," my father grunted. I relished how calm his voice was, even though I could sense the tension.

"It worked the first time, didn't it?" Dr. Nic returned.

Daddy didn't respond.

"You're welcome to admit it any time you like. You know. And I know who told you." Dr. Nic cursed. A few other voices I didn't recognize muttered along with him.

My father drew in a long breath and lowered his voice. "Just because it worked once doesn't mean it will work again. I don't think the United will buy another transit explosion."

He snarled in pain. Ephesus clenched his fists. I shut my eyes—and reached down to slide my reader back in my pouch.

"I'm creative. As soon as I find your brat of a daughter..."

I opened my eyes.

"I won't work on the project," Daddy interrupted. "Dead or alive."

Ephesus mouthed a prayer.

"I gathered that," Dr. Nic said coolly. "But you know too much."

There was scuffling. Daddy grunted. "Put him where Ephesus won't find him. Then search the base. I need to know where that rebel is before she realizes her father isn't coming back from his meeting. Be... discreet."

He embellished with a few swear words, but I didn't hear the rest. Ephesus punched the call button and whipped around, talking in hushed tones.

"We have one shot. We have to get you where Nic won't find you—if we can give him a chase, it'll buy us some time. Then—"

"Can we download some files to my reader? If we can get something up online, somewhere, it will alert the United."

He pondered that for a second, a split second too long. Before he could respond, the door whooshed open. Dr. Nic strode in, talking.

"Ephesus! I need—"

He glanced up and halted, for a brief second looking as shocked as we were. I stared back like a deer caught in headlights. Ephesus put a hand to his forehead as if to stabilize.

The tension shattered. Dr. Nic jerked upright and demanded, "How did you get in here?" He sounded a mix of enraged and curious.

I opened my mouth, then changed my mind. I stiffened and said with as much sass as I could muster, "I defy security."

He growled and looked on the verge of hitting me—or whatever was within reach. He drew his arm back.

Ephesus seemed to snap back to reality. "Don't touch her!" He lunged forward.

Dr. Nic turned and caught him in the shoulders. Ephesus crashed backwards, ramming his head on the table.

"You're in luck." Dr. Nic grabbed my arm and hauled me out of the room. "If the two of you behave, I'll pretend to kill you," he pinched my arm, "and your father, and you can stay here. If you pull stunts, legally dead won't be enough."

Ephesus staggered back to his feet. "Philli..."

Dr. Nic ignored him. He dragged me across the hall and shoved me into the half-finished meeting room.

I landed in a heap on the floor in the darkness. Dr. Nic toggled a few switches, and the lights flickered on. The panel glowed to life.

I sat up and stared at him. He crossed his arms calmly. "You have two choices. You can wait here for a few hours and live in peace with your father and brother for the rest of your life. Or you can make a ruckus and force me to decide how many of you I need to kill."

He took a step backwards, out of the room. He reached into the pocket of his lab coat and removed the reprogramming disc.

He set it on the panel and hit one button. The doors slid shut as he fiddled with a few other buttons.

The thought came to me so fast I barely had time to react. I jumped up and ran to the door just as it shut. Dr. Nic didn't notice. I stuck my hand over the inside panel and held it there.

The system chirped. A green circle glowed beneath my hand, as if winking conspiratorially. *The system can be set from either side of the door...*

I closed my eyes and praised God.

Shouts erupted in the hall. I hit the call button out of curiosity—it worked.

"Let her go!" Ephesus yelled.

"If you want me to kill her, I'd be happy to oblige."

There was silence. Dr. Nic continued. "I let you work on another phase; I can do the same with your father."

My whirlwind of thoughts crashed to a stop.

"No one has to die. You can stay and not have to work on Red Rain. All you have to do is be quiet for a few hours while I clean up your mess, and then it will be done."

I waited for Ephesus's response. He didn't give any. Dr. Nic grunted, "Smart choice. Carnegie!" Their footsteps retreated down the hall.

The speaker was silent for a minute. Two. Three. Now was my chance—my only chance.

I gazed at the panel. *You can wait here for a few hours and live in peace with your father and brother for the rest of your life.*

You can stay and not have to work on Red Rain.
All you have to do is be quiet...
I prayed—then waved my hand over the sensor.

26

The door opened willingly. I glanced in both directions and then stepped out into the halls, praising God.

I was out!

I locked the door behind me for good measure. I took two steps down the hall and spotted Gate A to my left. I stopped, stared at the letter, and moaned.

Well, I was halfway out. I was out of the room, but I wasn't out of Wing 74. And I wasn't going to be able to jump the system on that door.

I pinched my temples until I could feel the blood pounding beneath my fingers. This wasn't going to get me anywhere! I was just making things worse!

My nerves calmed in answer to prayer. No, it wasn't pointless. I still had my reader.

I needed to find a computer. One simple enough I could operate.

Like another reader.

I turned and ran for Lab 1. The door was open but the lights were off. My boot squeaked on the floor—and another footstep promptly answered it. Two voices approached down the hall—Dr. Nic and Carnegie.

I slapped my hand over my mouth to stifle a squeak. I skipped across the hall, hoping my footsteps were too faint to hear, and ducked around the door into the lab.

I knelt in the shadows under a table and pressed myself against the wall. I prayed they were just passing by. I closed my eyes so I could hear their voices better.

They were talking about me.

They weren't just passing by.

"I'm impressed with her boldness, actually," Carnegie said.

Dr. Nic sounded anything but impressed. "You'd think unassimilated would be more discreet and compliant." The footsteps stopped.

A pause. I cringed, waiting for the whoosh of the door and Dr. Nic's curses of anger.

I heard neither. Instead I heard a hideous, horrendous beep I knew all too well.

Access denied.

Something surged up my throat until it hurt. I opened my eyes.

Dr. Nic did swear. "What's wrong with this thing?"

Another beep. Another muttered breath. I eased towards the door.

"Didn't you set it?" Carnegie asked.

No... I did.

"Just now, when I locked her in." A third beep.

Hold your hands over the panel. One at a time, or it might mess the system up...

"I think that girl curses security systems wherever she goes." Carnegie sounded mildly amused.

Dr. Nic was far from it. For the third time, the only word to leave his mouth was foul. "I'll have to reset it." Footsteps retreated.

The disc. I stuck my head around the door in time to see Dr. Nic storm down the hallway.

Carnegie followed him at a more relaxed pace. "Didn't you just have it?"

"I left it on the desk!" They disappeared around the corner.

I jumped with excitement—literally. My foot smacked an empty glass bottle, sending it spiraling. I grabbed it just before it fell.

I shuddered. That would have been bad. Dr. Nic would have come running.

It hit me, like two magnets snapping together. With a million thoughts running through my head, I stood up too quickly.

I rammed my head on the underside of the table. Thankfully there was no glass on *top* of the table, and the only noise I produced was a faint thud.

I rubbed my hair, all the thoughts gone from my head except one. *Thank you, Lord.*

I eased out from under the table and stood up. The reader from Mr. Sardis was abandoned on the table in the middle of the room. I slid it in my pouch with my other reader and then shook the table. It shifted; it wasn't bolted to the floor. That would do.

I gazed at the chaos on the table. The various chemicals glowed surreal shades in the indirect light. *Not all the pieces are here, but you could create a disturbance.* Just what I needed.

But it wasn't enough. I glanced behind me and saw a closed door in the side wall.

I tried it. It opened. My brother must have had access.

Beyond was another lab, also deserted, with a door back to the hall. I opened it and looked around.

Carnegie's voice echoed, signaling their return. I backed into the shadows and watched them approach.

Dr. Nic, scowling bitterly, held out his hand. My heart leaped to see the reprogramming disc in his palm.

Everything was there. Everything was perfectly planned. But certainly not on account of any brilliance of mine.

I slid quickly along the wall, staying in the shadows, back into Lab 1. I stood next to the table, gripping it with both hands. I prayed for a burst of masculine strength.

I looked boldly out the door. It didn't matter if Dr. Nic glanced over his shoulder and saw me now. He'd be looking over his shoulder in a minute anyway.

The men stopped in front of the door. Dr. Nic reached out and held the disc over the panel.

I closed my eyes. When I heard the magnet click in place, I heaved.

Either the table was lighter than I expected, or God answered my prayer. Probably both. The table flew faster than I intended, causing me to jerk back with a little shriek.

Not that anyone but me could hear the shriek. The symphony of clattering metal and shattering glass was dazzling.

I cringed and threw my hands over my head instinctively—then remembered to run. I tripped over a pan and nearly fell through the door into the adjoining lab.

I was around the corner just in time. I heard Carnegie's unfinished "What the..." from the doorway.

Dr. Nic started yelling. "Argh... stop it!" Something crackled and sizzled. I took advantage of the noise to skip quickly out the door and into the hall.

The disc was waiting patiently for me on the panel. I snatched it and ran to Gate A. I didn't dare look back.

I snapped the disc onto the panel and raised my hand—then stopped.

How was I supposed to work this thing?

Panic and stupidity seized me—then bravery slapped it into silence. *You can do this. Just think. It can't be that hard. God, help me!*

I looked at the round device. It didn't have that many buttons. *This can't be that hard, this can't be that hard...*

The men's shouting disrupted my concentration. "Too late!" Carnegie screeched.

Dr. Nic hollered back, probably involuntarily. "Run!" They both obeyed. Frozen still, I looked back and watched them scramble out of the doorway.

Carnegie ran down the hall without looking in my direction. But Dr. Nic backed away slowly, staring into the room. I heard the crackling and sizzling grow louder now.

I knew what was going to happen a split second before he did it. The despair in my heart expected it.

Dr. Nic turned his head slightly and spotted me.

He whipped fully around in a blink. I couldn't move.

"You!" he snarled, which was what I expected him to say.

What I wasn't expecting was a sudden explosion to rock the lab, spewing a cloud of white smoke out into the hallway.

Suddenly I couldn't see Dr. Nic anymore. And he couldn't see me.

God had this more perfectly planned than I thought.

The smoke alarm went off, sending a wail and flashing lights coursing down the hall. No time to revel in perfection.

Coughing, I fanned smoke out of my face and hit a random button on the disc. Adrenaline was making my hand shake too much for me to be more precise.

Dr. Nic hacked. Someone—more than one someone?—shouted. But my ear was focused on the noise the panel was making.

It beeped. Then the doors slid open.

I glanced over my shoulder and saw Dr. Nic's hand emerge from the smoke like a monster rising from the grave. I snatched the disc and ran.

The doors eased shut behind me—too slowly. I saw Dr. Nic stand up, still coughing, just before the crack sealed. I waved my hand over the sensor and hoped that locked the door. I didn't wait to see.

I stumbled out of Gate 74 and locked it, too. I collapsed right where I was. I didn't have time to spare.

I yanked the readers out of my pouch and dropped the disc in their place. I tossed the reader from Mr. Sardis on the floor while it warmed up. I flipped mine over and pried the data chip out of the back.

The welcome screen on the Wing 74 device glowed. I picked it up and opened the main menu. Ephesus was right—a conglomeration of cryptic folders appeared.

I didn't have time to copy them all. What was most telltale?

I involuntarily grinned. Sliding the data chip in, I selected "Bible" and copied it. I picked a few other random important-looking folders.

The transfer bar filled quickly, but I was in such a rush that I almost yanked the chip out before the process was finished.

I shoved the chip in my reader and watched the bar climb again—slowly this time. My aged device choked at 30%.

"Please, God, please!" Then I remembered—getting them onto my device was only half the battle. They had to be where someone would see them.

I couldn't think of any websites I could access quickly enough. Nothing that was obvious. A United official had to see these files—now. How could I get ahold of a United official directly?

I smirked and opened my email. I started typing "Ambrose" and the system fed the appropriate address into the "to" field.

I tried to think of an eye-catching subject line. He had to read it, not glaze over and delete it like he did with most emails from criminals.

It came to me. *Subject: transmitting site*

Footsteps approached from the hall ahead. Friend or foe, I wasn't taking the risk.

No time to get cutesy with the message body. I typed: *Found a private database with Bibles and secret research. Send help. Philadelphia Smyrna*

I switched to the other window and found the copying finished. Praising God, I attached the files to the email and started the process all over again.

Gate 73 ahead of me opened. I looked up to see Cea enter. "Phil? What are you doing out here? How did…"

I looked back down at the screen. The last file began to load.

"What are you doing? What's going on?" She was on top of me.

Done. I hit send, and it went.

"Phil? Philli!"

I looked up at her. For an answer, I pulled the reprogram disc out of my pocket and held it up.

She gasped.

"It's over," I said. "It's over."

It truly was over.

Because two seconds later, a muffled explosion rocked the hall from behind. I instinctively dropped the reader and covered my head.

Two more explosions fired, the blast reverberating off the metal halls. Cea screamed and dropped to the ground.

Metal popped and cracked. I peered through my arms to see the walls buckle.

I heard the sound of electricity sparking. Cea screamed again, and I turned towards her—only to be knocked flat by something hitting my head. Glass shattered around me. I saw bright white, then darkness.

27

When I woke up, I didn't know where I was. It was too bright, too sterile. Nowhere I could remember being recently.

Fear, then panic, seized me. Something must have gone wrong. *Nic caught me again! Or... the explosion. The explosion went off, and I'm in the hospital, and everyone else is probably dead, and...*

Then I saw someone I recognized leaning over the bed. All other emotions left in favor of joy. "Ephesus!" I screeched and sat up.

He made a random noise of reproof and pushed me back. "Stay."

"Where's Dad? Are you okay?"

"Not so loud. I'm fine. Dad's talking with the officials."

I absorbed that information. My voice quieted. "You called them?"

"We didn't have to. They came with orders from Commander Ambrose."

I smiled and praised God.

Ephesus squeezed my hand. "I'm proud of you. That was quite the stunt."

"I didn't mean for it to blow up." The worry in my voice was real.

"What did you do?"

"Turned over the table in Lab 1."

He cringed. "I told you I was making a bomb."

"You said all the pieces weren't there!"

"Thankfully. Otherwise you would have killed all of us."

I pinched my eyes shut. *God had it all planned...*

I thought of something and sat up straight again. "Nic?"

Ephesus stared at me for a moment. "He'll heal. He was far enough away."

I closed my eyes and let out my breath. *Thank you, Lord.*

Ephesus gently pushed me down again. "You were pushing it, though. That close to the explosion, had you not been near an outside wall..."

I reached up and touched my neck. I felt a bandage across the back of it. "What happened?"

"Light fixture. A few cuts from the glass. It could have been a lot worse."

I flexed my arm and counted the small scrapes. "It would have been worth it."

Ephesus was quiet for a moment. "You ended Red Rain."

He stood up. "Rest. As soon as you're well enough, we're taking the first transit back to Earth."

He left, shutting off the light. I watched the low security lighting flicker on around the baseboards. I smiled into the darkness.

We were going home. All of us.

*

Daddy made me stay in bed until the morning, then we got up to pack. I was surprised to find the base nearly evacuated. Two

United officials guarded the dorms, and the rest of Wing 1 past the cafeteria was blocked off.

Red Rain—and all of Nic's operations—were over for good.

I was surprised when Mr. Sardis bumbled in to pick up our crates. He didn't look at us, just scooped up the luggage and hustled out.

"Sir!" I called after him. He stopped but didn't turn around.

I glanced at my father, then ventured, "Are you... coming on our flight?"

He shrugged. "I signed the file years ago."

He looked at me out of the corner of his eye, then left. My face fell. Daddy rubbed my shoulder.

We were waiting near the dock for our ride when I saw Cea. She breezed past the hallway and didn't glance in our direction.

"Cea!" I cried. She didn't stop.

I pounded to catch up with her. She ignored me. I squeezed past her in the hall and halted right in front of her, forcing her to stop.

She wouldn't look at me. I wasn't sure if I wanted to make eye contact. "I'm sorry," I said.

"You didn't mean for it to blow up." Her tone was cryptic, neither forgiving nor accusing.

"Nic?" I dared to ask.

"When he gets out of the hospital he'll have a home in jail." She pushed past me.

I didn't try to stop her. "Thank you," I called loud enough to be heard. She hesitated at the turn. "For being honest."

She left.

Commander Ambrose was neither pleased nor displeased to see us back, though to his credit he pretended not to be surprised by Ephesus's return from the dead.

Our neighbors at the camp were a different story. I couldn't remember the last time a new arrival in camp had been a cause for celebration.

I was surprised at how happy I was to go to school again, to ride on the bus with Cami and Aid and listen to my teacher's rants. Daddy still waited for the bus with me, only this time Ephesus stood with us.

The only thing that was missing was Mr. Dass's arguments. He didn't come out of his house much anymore. Cami said they hadn't heard a word from Mira or Stanyard since they left.

I made a note to pray for them more often. Their names went right below Cea's.

It was on the bus ride to school that Cami reminded me what I had left behind on Mars.

"Do you still have the file?"

I gasped and reached for my pouch—then remembered it wasn't there. I hadn't put it on because I didn't have anything to go in it.

I'd left both readers on the floor in the wreckage by Wing 74. I hadn't been allowed to go back and collect them.

I abruptly grinned. I knew who had a copy. "Ephesus has one on his computer."

I bombarded him as soon as I came home from school. He stared at me for a long moment before shaking his head.

"What?"

"They confiscated all the computers from Wing 74 for evidence."

I covered my face. Ephesus reached out and touched my shoulder. "Didn't you send a copy to Commander Ambrose?"

I looked up at him and smiled.

Daddy transferred our query the next day. The response he got was "no transmitting."

I cried into his shoulder when he told me. Ephesus spoke up. "Someone will upload a copy sooner or later. I'm helping them patch the virus."

"God will find a way," Dad repeated.

I sat up. "He preserved the Bible through the virus." I looked at Ephesus.

He smiled sadly. "With Wing 74."

Daddy squeezed my hand. "With Wing 74."

28

A few days later, the bus dropped me off on the wrong street. It couldn't go down my row because Ambrose's car was blocking the road.

I jumped off the bus, listening to the driver complain about conflicting schedules. As the bus drove away, I walked down the sidewalk and tried to see what the commotion was.

A guard carried a crate up the steps of one of the vacant houses. New people.

I ventured closer to the house, looking for the unfamiliar faces and wondering if they'd want to be greeted. Sometimes new convicts didn't want to talk to anyone for weeks.

Commander Ambrose was talking with someone on the sidewalk. The guard came out of the house and climbed into the car. Nodding curtly, Ambrose followed in suit, leaving the new resident alone on the sidewalk.

I recognized her.

"Cea!" I ran for her—then stopped, confusion overtaking my joy.

She turned in my direction and stared stoically at me.

I crept closer. "Are you…?"

"I came to return what's yours."

"And you had to bring all your belongings with you?"

I could see the smile tugging at her lips now. She reached into her bag and pulled something out.

My reader. She pressed it upside down in my hand. I stared at the scuffed case for a minute before flipping it over and looking at the screen.

It was on. Revelation was loaded.

I know your deeds. See, I have placed before you an open door that no one can shut. I know that you have little strength, yet you have kept my word and have not denied my name.

I threw my arms out and hugged her.

"Thank you," she whispered in my ear.

I stood at arm's length. "Welcome home."

She smiled.

TO BE CONTINUED…

PROJECT
74

RED RAIN #1.5
RACHEL NEWHOUSE
& DAVID HARTUNG

THERE'S MORE TO THE STORY...

Ephesus waited until twenty minutes before curfew before venturing back to the lab.

Even though he would have appreciated the cover of darkness, he didn't want to raise additional suspicion by being out after the hallway lights automatically dimmed to save power. Thankfully, almost everyone else seemed to have retired for the night, and he passed no one.

Casting one last fugitive glance around the halls, he approached the lab and swiped his hand over the panel. He cringed at how loud the shrill *access granted* beep seemed in the silence.

He slipped through the doors before they were even all the way open and shut them again, locking them for good measure. At least this lab didn't have any windows.

Even so, he didn't dare turn the lights on. The low security lighting around the baseboards was enough to guide him through the chaos of equipment to the computer station at the back of the room.

Ephesus tapped the screen and winced as it flashed on at full brightness. He quickly toggled keys to dim it to an appropriate level.

He stared at the login screen, trying to swallow the nagging feeling that he was breaking and entering. He reminded himself why he had to know, rehearsing all his questions and concerns until the burning desire to understand drowned out his fear.

Ephesus slowly typed in Nic's username and password, his fingers barely touching the keys, as though he were afraid to leave fingerprints.

He glanced up at the screen, where a string of dots represented the password. The "submit" button glowed red.

"I hope this is the right thing to do," he muttered, and hit enter.

He braced himself as the screen loaded. Subconsciously he expected something catastrophic to happen—for an alarm to go off, or maybe something horrible and nightmarish would appear on the screen. He was almost disappointed when he peeked out and saw a mundane list of files.

They all had mundane file names and mundane file extensions. Ephesus scanned the list and easily interpreted the contents. He was used to deciphering lab notes. There was some research, some lab results, some reports from bomb-testing grounds...

Ephesus stopped. There were weapon test reports here. He had seen these kinds of reports once or twice on Earth, when he had been involved with a project that required explosives and projectiles to be tested in a secure area. What would Dr. Nic be making that required explosive testing? And where in the world was he doing that testing? In all his traversing, Ephesus hadn't seen any areas on the base that would be suitable for testing explosives.

Unless it was in the one area of the base he didn't have full access to.

Wing 74.

He hovered his finger over one of the weapon test reports. Maybe Earth was contracting Dr. Nic to test weapons. After all, Mars was probably an ideal place to conduct explosive testing, especially out here at base #9.6.11. There was nothing but craters of red dirt for miles. The perfect place to drop a few bombs.

Ephesus lowered his hand. It wasn't really his business to worry about it. His assignment didn't involve any weapons. Why did he care what the other scientists up here were working on?

But then again, he was being asked to make an acidic compound for another phase of the project. And Dr. Nic hadn't been too eager to tell him what the compound was for.

It could very well be for a weapon. And if that was the case, the result would be one *extremely* lethal weapon.

Ephesus tapped the file to open it.

AVAILABLE NOW!

CROOK O

RED RAIN #2
RACHEL NEWHOUSE

AND IT ISN'T OVER YET...

The knock came during dinner.

Ephesus answered the door. He had barely pulled it open before three armed guards shoved their way inside.

"May I help you?" Ephesus yelped indignantly, stumbling back.

The soldiers spread themselves in the entryway and halted. "We have orders to take two unassimilated citizens into special custody," the captain of the group declared.

I gasped, a sound which seemed gratingly loud in the sudden silence. For a moment it seemed the only thing moving in the entire room was my panicked heart.

Special custody... two unassimilated...

"What?" Ephesus yelled, more as an exclamation of shock than a question.

Dear God, no.

The captain ignored him. He scanned the room, his eyes coming to rest just above my head. I knew in my heart that he was looking at Daddy, who was standing behind me.

Please no...

I didn't have time to finish the prayer before the captain confirmed my fears. "You're under arrest."

God, no! Please don't take my father and brother away. Not again!

I whipped around to look at Daddy, silently begging him to tell me it wasn't true. Shock and fear briefly flashed across his eyes, but he let it out with a sigh. Straightening, he said with brave calmness, "Will you allow us to gather a few belongings first?"

The captain nodded. "Ten minutes."

Daddy turned towards the stairs. I yearned to cry out after him, but I couldn't find any words.

Ephesus stayed where he was and sputtered, "What is the meaning of this?"

The captain finally looked at him. "The reasons for her arrest are confidential."

Silence again iced over the room. This time my heart stopped altogether.

"Her?" Ephesus repeated.

Daddy stopped at the bottom of the stairs and glanced back.

"Yes," the captain said slowly, as if he didn't understand what the confusion was. "She's the one under arrest."

The statement was accompanied by a flick of his hand at me.

AVAILABLE NOW!

WANT EXCLUSIVE BONUS SCENES?

Become a Patron and get access to **exclusive bonus scenes** for this series! This bonus content is not available anywhere else, and I post a new scene every month. Plus, you can get digital ARCs, signed paperbacks, collector's edition hardbacks, and merch, or read my WIP as I write it!

Become a Patron at:
patreon.com/rachelnewhouse

Or sign up for my newsletter and be the first to hear about new releases—plus get sneak peeks of upcoming books, cover art, and more!

Sign up at:
rachelnewhouse.com/subscribe

DID YOU LOVE THIS BOOK?

Please consider leaving a review on Amazon or Goodreads! It's one of the most important things you can do to support an indie author. Thank you!

HI FROM RACHEL

Rachel Newhouse is an author, wife, secretary, and Sunday school teacher from Kansas City, Missouri. Her obsessions are sci-fi, dystopian, and kid lit. When she's not writing, she's cooking Asian food, growing chilis that are too spicy to eat, and watching wildly age-inappropriate shows like *My Little Pony* and *Gravity Falls* with her husband, Joe. She also really likes glitter. You've been warned.

Connect with Rachel:
bio.site/rachelnewhouse